The Celebration
Paul Melniczek

The Celebration

Paul Melniczek

King's Way Press

Atlanta 2017

King's Way Press

3721 New Macland Rd.
Suite 200-141 Powder
Springs, GA 30157
http://www.kwp-
books.com

ISBN-13: 978-0-9988367-6-8
ISBN-10: 0-9988367-6-1

The Celebration

Paul Melniczek

The Celebration

Shington, Halloween Night, 1975

The car swerved around the curve, the tires screeching loudly in protest. Nick looked in the rearview mirror, knowing that he'd really done it this time. The stakes were raised, and the chase was on. Going to prison had never seemed too appealing, but the reality of seeing it firsthand loomed before him. There was no sneaking out of this one…it was either full throttle, or face the music.

Swearing, he saw a flash somewhere behind him. Distant yet, but too close for comfort. And if he knew these bastards, they would chase him across the county line if necessary. Actually, he did know them pretty damn well by now. Focusing on the road ahead, he felt the back tires lurch, skimming over fallen leaves which were slick from an earlier shower. He needed to maintain control, or else he would bite it into a tree

7

trunk or a side rail. If he could just stay far enough ahead, at least until he made it over the Wyming Creek Bridge, then there was a decent chance of escape on the broader highway which led out of town. And this time it would be for good.

He passed a log cabin to his right, ignoring the trio of pumpkins which sat at the end of the driveway. Normally he would have smirked, stopping by to heave the orange blobs into the trees, or smash them where they sat. Kid stuff, but fun.

At the moment he was a little too busy...

The night passed him by, and he felt a mixture of raw emotions. Exhilaration and fear from the chase, satisfaction that he'd ruined the evening for so many people, and also a surge of hope, that he could finally put this dump behind him and move on to greener pastures. Maybe Hook up with his brother Carson soon. Hell, they could get into some serious action together. But first, he needed to lose the cops. Nick was full of confidence that he could outrun them and leave his pursuers burning in the dust with his blue Nova matched against their cruiser, which had seen its better days.

"Whoa..."

The car slid around a bend and he knew that the bridge was close. He handled the vehicle smoothly, enjoying the rush of adrenalin brought on by high speed. He would show them all how stupid they really were, and he was through being pushed around by anyone. Those days were over. He'd outsmarted them every step of the way, and now, on Halloween night, it was coming to an end.

Just like he'd planned all along. The perfect night for his perfect scheme.

The Celebration

Another quarter of a mile raced by, and he was startled as something jumped into the road in front of him. Never slowing, he clocked it in the side, watching as it flailed away, crushed by his bumper. He couldn't tell if it had been a dog or other small animal, and he didn't care. "Ten points for me." He chuckled without remorse.

Suddenly the road opened before him and the bridge appeared. He thought back to the story of Sleepy Hollow where the Headless Horseman couldn't pursue Ichabod any further, and to Nick, it looked like his own personal gateway to freedom at the moment. Well, not quite, but the odds were shifting toward his side. Soon he could let it rip and give the Nova its head to blister down the highway and leave the cops behind.

His window was open several inches and the air felt cool and refreshing against his face. He reached the bridge, hearing the familiar clang of rubber over grid, and was halfway over when a blast echoed from outside. Immediately the car swerved to the right, and he fought to keep it away from the edge, his stomach tightening into knots as the front of the Nova smacked into the rail with crushing force. Pulling with all his strength, he tried desperately to regain control, but his speed was too great, the momentum of the car unstoppable.

The car broke through the protective railing and leaned heavily to the right, and *downwards*. The world immediately reversed to Nick's frightened vision and he felt a sickening drop, worse than any amusement ride he had ever experienced, as the car nosedived into the ice cold river below. The impact was quick and powerful, Nick's head smashing into the windshield, his neck twisting into an impossible angle.

The chase was over, the moon casting a silver glint onto the blasted ruin of metal far below.

Paul Melniczek

The Celebration

October 1ˢᵗ, Seven Years Later

When Cal got the phone call from Mary Wilkinson, he gently hung up the receiver as he looked out his office window, the brisk morning clouding over. He was disturbed by the conversation, more so than he cared to admit.

Mary had called in a complaint of vandalism. All of her outdoor Halloween decorations had been completely demolished. Several pumpkins, some blow molds, and a homemade ghost, given to her by Shelly, her granddaughter. That last one had stung the most. Cal had promised the woman that he would be over later that morning, or send one of his men, and a full report would follow.

He stood up from his chair, taking a sip from his coffee mug, tasting the black 'TNT' as he called it. Looking out the window, his eyes ran over the distant outline of the Shington Elementary schoolyard, as he reminisced about his own childhood days. Now in his early forties, they seemed like the dreams from another lost lifetime. Where did the years go? It was crazy how time moved on. He felt a sudden rush of sadness, nostalgia and memory fragments taking hold and sweeping him away momentarily. It was always around the holidays when the feelings were strongest. For some reason, the memories were more vivid, the scenes playing over and over in his head like an old projection film. Maybe it was from all the familiar trappings surrounding the holiday, things that could be recalled more easily because you experienced some of the same things every year. Pumpkins, witches, black cats, trickor-treating and scary costumes. Holidays stood out because they broke up the monotony of a daily routine. It made a lot of sense.

And speaking of routines, he had business to take care of. But first, he needed to stop his stomach from growling.

Cal left his office, talking for a moment with Ann, his secretary, and then he headed out, driving the short distance to Miller's Diner, which served as the center of town in more ways than one. Serving up bacon and eggs just as quickly as all the local gossip, it was a hub ring for the citizens to gather and spread the word, whatever it was -- good or bad. The sheriff entered, nodding to familiar faces as he sat down on a stool, sliding a menu into his palms. The walls were decked out in fifties style, complete with car bumpers on either end of the table area. He glanced over the offerings, mumbling to himself.

"Hey Mr. Policeman." A waitress came over, and he looked up. "What will it be, the regular?"

"Morning, Rachel. Yeah, the blacker the better."

"Okee dokee. How are you doing today?"

The Celebration

"Oh, just peachy," he replied. "On my way to check out some Halloween pranks, that's about it. Kids, what can you say…"

The waitress leaned over the counter, and Cal tried not to look down her low-cut blouse. Rachel was around his age, take off a few years, of medium height, a full-figured brunette moving steadily to plump, although not unpleasantly so. She bent over lower, as if deliberately trying to draw his eyes to where she wanted him to look.

No, he thought. *Don't even go there.* "Hungry this morning?" she asked.

"Sure. How about a pair of eggs scrambled, with bacon and ham on the side?"

Rachel pursed her lips. "All right, cowboy. Anything you want." Winking, she walked away, and Cal dropped his head fully into the steaming cup of coffee, ignoring the extra swagger she put into her hips; one meant especially for him.

He pictured his wife Mindy in his mind then, unconsciously, comparing the two. Where Rachel was sultry and seductive, his wife was quiet and classy, a natural beauty whose shyness made her even more attractive. He felt a twinge of guilt, immersing himself in the dark liquid. He tried to banish the wanderings of his mind, instead focusing on the day's activities. Mary Wilkinson's place was his next stop. He wanted to see for himself what had happened, and who the likely suspect would be. Why, there hadn't been any major Halloween pranks in a while. Years, in fact. So it bothered him more than a little to hear about something like this.

And October was only beginning, the big day still weeks away.

Paul Melniczek

A half hour later found the sheriff over at Mary Wilkinson's place, a corner lot rancher on Maple Street. It was a pleasant enough neighborhood, quiet, with lots of trees and hedgerows, most of the homes aging gracefully, some more than others. In the distant background were the lands of Farmer Stock, huge rows of corn sweeping into the horizon as far as you could see.

Standing in her front yard, Cal examined the damage. Pumpkin shards lay scattered everywhere, the orange husks thrown about as if blown up by dynamite. Plastic decorations were ripped apart, unsalvageable, but worst of all was the ghost made by her granddaughter -- a homemade construction of sheets and paper mache with two blinking eyes -- which Mary had hung from a tree bough for effect. It had been neatly sliced apart by a knife, cut into strips so small you could have made shoestrings out of them.

Despite the ugliness, it was the handiwork of someone who knew what they were doing, regardless of the intent.

"What a terrible thing for someone to do. I want them caught and punished, sheriff."

"I'll be on it immediately. Don't worry."

Mary frowned, clearly upset. She pulled her wool jacket tightly about her gaunt frame, shaking her head.

"Why would anyone do such a thing? It makes no sense, none at all. My poor Shelly will be so upset, the dear child. And I just put all this stuff out." The elderly woman looked on the verge of tears.

"Why don't you work on a new prop with her? It will take your mind off what happened here," Cal offered. "There's no need to let one idiot spoil everything else."

"You're right, I suppose." Mary sighed. "Still…"

"We'll find out who it was. Just give us some time to do our work."

Mary nodded, but the woman looked unconvinced.

"I'll be in touch. And I'll have an extra patrol cruise down your street at night. You might want to keep things inside the house until we catch the culprit."

"What's *left* of it all, you mean. Oh, what's the world coming to," Mary said. "Such nastiness. You know, it reminds me of…"

Cal cut her off. "I have to run. Take care." "Thank you, sheriff. And make sure you catch whoever did this. Make them pay."

He nodded, turning away and heading back to his car. He opened the door and sat for a minute, writing some notes on a clipboard and taking sips from his coffee cup. He felt a bit distracted, and his mind kept wandering. He thought about October, and how the town embraced the harvest season, ultimately leading to what was called The Celebration, a big festival which took place in the center of town, where merchants sold baked goods, kids dressed in costume, and the town created a family- friendly environment which included trappings of both the harvest season and Halloween alike.

Shington was a small town, so it ended up being a big deal, although some of the residents took the opportunity to celebrate a bit *too* much, usually in the form of hard liquor and public drunkenness. As a matter of fact, it could turn out to be more trouble than it was worth, which was a shame.

He shook his head, finishing his paperwork. The sky remained clouded over, and he looked up, his green eyes gazing across the neighborhood. From the corner of his vision, he spotted movement between the large hedgerows which separated two of Mary's neighbors. It looked as if someone -- or something -- had moved deeper into the bush. He stared at the spot for long moments, wondering if his eyes were playing tricks. It was a bit gloomy out, and the morning was only half gone, but still.

Could the culprit be lurking nearby? It would be extremely foolish for someone to stick around and admire their handiwork, especially if the police were on the scene investigating.

Foolish or brash...

Shaking his head, Cal finished up the paperwork, giving the hedgerow one last glimpse before heading off, convinced that it had been nothing.

It was only after the police cruiser had turned the corner and moved out of sight, that something stirred inside the hedgerow again.

The Celebration

Later that evening, Cass Andrews stood behind the garage which served as her living quarters. Her mom lived in the main house, but she preferred the privacy of the separate building, as opposed to being near Clint, her mom's live-in boyfriend, and all-around loser type of guy.

Corn fields were everywhere, and a long line of trees cut straight through their dried forms, serving as boundary between adjoining properties. The air was cool, the night clear, and Cass loved it all. The freshness, the feeling of isolation, and most importantly, the season.

She was a child of the fall, of darkness, of Halloween. She had always known this, always accepted it. Dressed in a black jacket and dark jeans, her small feet glided across the ground like a wraith as she took in her surroundings, enjoying the moment. She didn't like people, and was a natural loner, having no true friends. And the only one she'd ever felt close to was gone.

"Nick."

She whispered into the air, the breeze clutching at the tree branches, making them quiver. Often she called out to him, hoping for an answer, but the night was always quiet. Nick had left a long time ago, the one person who could have taken her away from this place, added excitement to her life, promising adventure.

Gone.

The tears had dried up years ago, but she still clung to his memory. She still couldn't believe it. October always brought her closer to the fateful date, closer to him. Ironically, their own feelings about the night had been strangely opposite. She had always adored Halloween while Nick considered it just another opportunity for making trouble.

Cass walked towards the nearest cornstalk, her hand caressing the dried husk. It felt so fragile, as if she could crumble it into a fine powder if she so desired. *Life* was fragile, and every breath you took could be your last. Nick's loss had changed her forever, and she had never looked at the world the same ever since. Her own routine was boring, as she worked at the small knitting mill, keeping to herself and her own dark thoughts.,

Black hair tousled by the wind, she moved a long strand from her face with one hand. She was a pretty girl, but there were few who would admit it, unable to get past the solemn expression, dark outfits, and reserved demeanor. It was a small town, and people didn't forget. Nick had left permanent scars here, and Cass had been his girlfriend.

They didn't forget, and some would never forgive.

Behind her, candles flickered in the windows, the wicks dancing from hidden drafts. This area was her domain, her frontier. She felt comfortable here, alone, and bothered by no one. She looked up into the sky, admiring the clouds which clustered overhead, but she jumped in surprise as something touched her back. Snapping around, her eyes darkened when she saw Clint's leering face.

Well, maybe not bothered by no one.

"Scared you?" He chuckled, his hand still resting on her shoulder.

Cass slumped down, backing away and trying to shake off his unwanted touch. "Leave me alone. You have no right to sneak up on me."

"Just trying to keep you company until your mom gets back. You never know who might be skulking around out here." "No, I think I know quite well who might be doing just that."

"Still got a mouth on you, girl. After all these years, you haven't changed one damn bit." "Get out of here. And stay away from me." Clint moved closer. "Oh, come on now. Wouldn't you like a bit of company some time? Have a real man around?"

"There are no real men in this town. Only a bunch of hopeless hicks going nowhere fast."

She glared at him in defiance, but she felt nervous, trying her hardest not to show it. Cass had no idea what her mom saw in this loser, but more likely than not had turned a blind eye to his many shortcomings. And right now he reeked of whiskey.

"Like that stupid old boyfriend of yours? You still can't let him go. Your mom told me all about you two. You're wasting your life, you know. Living in the past. Why don't you have a little fun for once?" His grin was nasty, and Cass saw the lust in his eyes.

"I'll tell my mom about you…"

"You'll do *what*?" He loomed before her, his face turning deadly serious. "You think she has any reason to believe you at all, you little bitch? All that black you wear all the time, and dark makeup? No friends, no life. Who knows what else you're up to, hanging out here at night by yourself."

"Get away from me."

She moved to her left but Clint was too fast, grabbing her arm and squeezing. "You like it rough? Like your mom, maybe?"

"Pig…" She slapped him away, but they both turned as they heard the hum of an engine coming from the front of the house. Clint laughed. "She's home early. Too bad. How about a rain check?"

"You *ever* touch me again and I swear you'll pay. I'll go to my mom and the sheriff."

Clint paused, as if considering her threat. "You really want to go there? I doubt you have the nerve." Shrugging, he walked away.

Cass felt dirty from his touch, shuddering. Relieved that her mother had returned, she was still shaken, wishing that the woman would finally wake up and see what kind of a man she was shacking up with. Shaking her head, she moved back into the deeper shadows, wondering how long it would be until Clint followed through with his advances. It might happen one day soon. He'd grown bolder recently, as if her mom's mental decline only added to his arrogance. She'd hit the bottle in a big way lately, and showed no signs of slowing. Cass missed the closeness they'd once shared, but knew that the connection had no chance of being strengthened while Clint was around.

She stared into the darkness, wishing things would be better, wishing that Nick was still here. Clint had been right about one thing at least. Her obsession with him was as strong as ever.

The Celebration

Cass returned to the garage where she had placed a pair of jack-o-lanterns to either side of the doorway. An old rocking chair sat to the right of the small porch. She eased into it, feeling the night and trying to seek out its mysteries. Her body tingled with energy, fresh off the encounter with Clint. She felt the blood surging through her veins, swept up in a moment of passion that she didn't fully understand. She had tried hard to keep Nick's memory alive. Keep *him* alive. If there were some way to bring him back, she would have gladly done anything to make it a reality. And Nick would have dealt with Clint, put that creep in his place. Cass reached down, caressing the living skin of the pumpkin, admiring the cool texture beneath her palms. She'd carved wicked teeth into it, with a triangular nose and circular top to light a candle inside. Reaching into her pocket, she pulled out a lighter, illuminating one, then the other. Satisfied, she sat there, gently rocking back and forth, collecting her thoughts and letting the night have its way with her imagination.

Clint.

If only there was a way to get him out of the picture. *And* the others in town who looked down on her. What a bunch of self-righteous hypocrites. They all had their imperfections, but if someone looked or acted a little different? Whispers and laughter behind your back. Quiet, but enough that they didn't fool her. She wished they could all be taught a lesson and would never mock her again as she passed by.

The jack-o-lanterns gleamed menacingly in the dark, the cavernous eyes sparkling with malice and contempt.

A perfect match for her own grim stare.

Cal looked down over the ridge, admiring the parade of colorful trees which enveloped the valley. Burnt orange and red, fading yellows, and hybrid shades alike, all combining to paint a quintessential portrait of a landscape caught up in autumn's grand scheme.

It was a beautiful sight, and one that he never grew tired of, not until his last breath. It was one of the reasons he loved the town and the area, and knew there was nothing here that would ever cause him to leave.

Not even the guilt he felt.

Turning, he heard footsteps approaching from behind, watching as a large shape materialized from the forest.

"Stand's in decent shape yet. A couple of loose nails. I'll be up in a few days and hammer them in." Jake Saddle, Cal's lead deputy, stomped a heavy boot into a rotten tree stump, shaking dirt off in tiny clumps.

"Good," Cal replied. "I haven't seen that big one around lately, but I know he's still up here. Did you see that buck rub down the trail, oh, maybe a hundred yards back?"

"No, but I believe you. He's been up here for years. Got a shot at him once, but that's a while back now. Sonofabitch is one trophy stud, though. A regular king of the mountain here. His antlers will look good over my mantle."

"If you ever land him, which I doubt."

"I'll get him, sooner or later. Even if it's off season."

"No you won't." Cal raised his eyebrows.

"Aw, c'mon. Who's ever going to know?"

The Celebration

"Me, for one. And Harry, for another. Bringing in a deer to his shop after the season's over. That won't look too good. If I catch you poaching, you'll be losing your license courtesy of *me*."

Jake shook his head. "You know, you could live it up a little sometimes. You *are* the law around here."

"Exactly, so I try to lead by example. And I do pull a few strings now and then, mostly to keep *you* out of trouble."

The deputy shrugged, looking unconcerned.

"How are you coming with the leads about Mary Wilkinson's place?" Cal asked, changing the subject.

"Not much. But there's been another incident."

"Oh? Why didn't you tell me?"

"Well, on your day off, I didn't want to bother you."

"I don't have any days off. So what is it?"

"Marlene Seller's dog is missing."

"Yeah, that happens. Broken chain, or what?"

"Nope. They heard barking sometime after midnight, which is nothing unusual from that mutt. In the morning, the dog was gone. The chain had been untied from the tree, and all their pumpkins from their front porch were smashed. There's more. Every single one from their garden was chopped up into little pieces. And you know how big their garden is…they sell a bunch every year. Nothing left. They're really upset. About both."

"I can see why."

"You're thinking what I'm thinking, of course." Jake nodded. "They're connected. Some punk is out there going overboard for Halloween. Smashing pumpkins is one thing. But taking a dog moves everything up a level."

"We need to move on this quick. I'll take a drive over there later. Day off or not. We had one really bad year and it started the same time as all this, and I'm going to make damn sure nothing like *that* ever happens again…"

"Exactly."

"It might be one hell of a long shot, but we should look into Ronald Skewer. He's been getting into a lot of trouble at school."

They both stood there in silence, gazing down over the quiet valley, lost in their own thoughts.

Cal looked outside as Mindy placed pumpkins on their front porch, carefully arranging them at the bottom of a pair of corn stalks. A few days into October, and it seemed like summer had already been long forgotten. The neighborhood was changing tone. Trees were full of color, and homes were putting on a mantle of orange and black, their residents moving steadily into the autumn season. Fallen leaves swept dreamily across their lawn, and several piles were scattered about like miniature hills, waiting to be placed in the gutter. He had started his own cleanup, but things kept interrupting his house work.

More calls into the office complaining of vandalism…

The door opened and Mindy walked inside, followed by Rex, their chocolate lab.

"Wow! The air smells so clean. The weather always seems to know what month it is." She smiled at him, a few strands of her honey wheat hair a bit out of place. A few years his junior, she still looked no older than thirty.

He grinned back, but the gesture felt empty. "I'll try to get on the rest of the front yard, but it won't be until later. The office called, and I have to get back in there."

She nodded. "I'm not too busy. I might have to go into the flower shop later. Shirl asked me to help with a new shipment that just came in."

"Yeah," he asked?

Trying to pay attention, it was difficult, his mind distracted by so many things lately. October was full of memories, and not all of them pleasant. As the days grew shorter and the nights longer, the past reared up in the background, growing in strength and trying to capture his focus. It wasn't an easy task, trying to balance everything and keep things in perspective. Cal considered himself a decent person, but living with guilt had been a lot harder than he had ever thought.

"You all right? You look distracted." "I'm fine. Just a lot of stuff going on around town, and I need to get to the bottom of it. Part of the job. Someone's got to do it."

"And they keep reminding you all the time."

Nodding, Cal moved over and kissed her lightly on the cheek. "See ya' later, hon."

She gave him a quick hug, and moved into the dining room, Cal's eyes never leaving the gentle sweep of her shoulders. He went through the front door, going outside, and then stopped. Retracing his steps, he took out his key, making sure to lock it, something he normally wouldn't have worried about. Not in this neighborhood, not in Shington. But now…

25

A chill went up his spine, partly from the wind, and also from the feeling of anxiety which had been plaguing him the past several days. The air had changed recently, and something nasty was stirring, making its way throughout the town in subtle fashion, showing itself just a bit, but getting bolder.

Something had to be done. And soon.

He walked across the lawn toward the side driveway and his cruiser which was parked in front of the garage, and he glanced over its brick exterior. It served to house one of their vehicles at any given time, and he used it as storage for yard and work projects. It also had an upper loft where Mindy kept household spillover items and a few odds and ends. The single window stared blankly at him, appearing dark and vacant. The glass looked cold, and the frame was in need of a fresh coating of paint. Just another task to put on his list, he thought. One that was growing longer by the day.

Sighing, he entered the car, firing it up. There was so much going on at the moment, especially now that Mayor Sam Winston was in Florida. Speculation was that the man was looking at real estate, thinking ahead to an early retirement. With him gone, everything seemed to fall into his own lap now, adding on to his police duties with administrative questions. He had always worked well with Sam, but the Mayor's secretary, Jenn, was not one for decision making, no matter how trivial it was. She constantly was calling the sheriff and asking him what to do. Showing her a lot of patience, he had long passed the point where he could refuse offering his opinion. Things would become a mess real quick if he avoided her. Sam had no full-time staff besides her, and the town had managed well enough on its streamlined leadership. The budget didn't allow for much more, truth be told. So Cal accepted his role of leadership, despite the rumblings that Mayor Winston was leaving soon, and a replacement would be needed.

And of course Cal had heard the other rumors of who *that* might be, something he didn't necessarily relish.

Himself.

Cruising along the side streets, he arrived at the station, barely remembering the short drive, his mind preoccupied. The sidewalks were deserted as he walked to the back of the building, going through the unlocked door.

"Sheriff, another call."

Arlene waved over to him as soon as he entered, and Cal frowned. "Yeah, what do we have now?"

"Ray Sherke wants to meet you over at the cemetery soon as you can. He'll be there all afternoon working."

"Ray? What in the world could he want? Did he say what was so important?"

Arlene's face was expressionless, as normal. "Vandalism."

Cal felt a shiver going down his back. *Man,* he thought. Something bad had happened over at the Shington Cemetery, where Ray was the caretaker. There was no doubt about it. *Was nothing sacred anymore?*

"I'll take care of it shortly."

"He's called twice already. And he said he would be calling back soon."

"I've been a little busy." Cal was irritated. "If he calls back again, tell him I'll be over today. I don't want any direct calls."

"All right. There's some fresh coffee in the pot. Sounds like you might need some right now."

"Bullseye."

Cal stalked down the short hallway and went into his office, which seemed like a sanctuary at the moment. Being a police officer in a small town, one expected a mix of problems, and many days of complete boredom. He didn't mind challenges, as long as people weren't getting hurt or property damaged, but lately things had taken a sharp spiral downwards, with pranks and vandalism escalating. The townspeople were becoming nervous, and that wasn't a good sign. Agitated people could sometimes do rash things, like lashing out at others, or start accusing someone without any proof of guilt. Right now, there were no witnesses to the malicious activities, and maybe a handful of possible suspects. A few seconds later Arlene poked her head inside with the pitcher of promised coffee. He nodded absently to her, and after filling his mug she left, closing the door behind her. The woman knew her place in the office without asking, and it was one of the things Cal liked about her. She could read his moods like a book, and tried her best not to become a nuisance. Not that he was hard to work for, but everyone had their moments.

The sheriff sipped from his mug, leaning back, and turning in the swivel chair. Jake had second shift today and was out patrolling the streets of the town. Marlin had night, and that left first patrol to Josh, although they rotated shifts and hours. Including him, they were the entirety of the town's police force, which gave little leeway for anything needing extra attention. Of course, all of the investigative duties fell on his shoulders, and that was the way it worked. Jake was assigned to whatever Cal felt like giving him, and although the guy had a rough edge, would do as told.

The Celebration

Ultimately, it was Cal who was responsible for keeping Shington and its people safe. And if the problems continued without the culprit being found, he would hear a lot more complaints, and many of them would be directed at *him.*

Shuffling through papers, he knew this would be only a brief respite before he went out to the cemetery. He was already anxious to see what was going on over there, and his gruffness illustrated his frustration in not being able to solve the growing amount of pranks.

"Ah well."

He sat up from the desk, going over to the window. The sky had darkened the past half hour, and he knew that thunderstorms were in the area. The temperature had grown warmer and more humid the past hour, as a quickly-moving front had moved in. He stared over at the elementary school, watching as children were ushered inside by their teachers. Whether the recess period was over or from fear of the storms, Cal didn't know, but soon the play area was empty. He watched as one of the swings shifted without an occupant. It looked odd to him, but he blamed it on the breeze, which had picked up from the unstable air pattern. For one brief second he had a vision of a youth wearing a black jacket swinging back and forth on the swing, staring silently at him. Shaken by the image, the vision quickly vanished and there was nothing to be seen out there except a melancholy schoolyard surrounded by trees with quivering limbs.

Cal blinked his eyes several times.

Too many things going on lately, he told himself. *And the ugliness needed to stop, the culprit brought into the station.*

And soon.

Paul Melniczek

Before he knew it, Cal was off once more and driving through town, making several stops which stole away the waning afternoon, so by the time he neared the Shington Cemetery it was much later than he expected. The cemetery sat at the far edge of town in the spot everyone called the Nook. The area had been given its name because of the tight valley where it lay, surrounded on three sides by gently sloping foothills which cupped about it like the hands of an immense giant. The sheriff pulled up to the front gate, which had seen its better years. Rust ran along the length, and clumps of bushes followed the outline until it faded into the tree line. Cal paused as he left the vehicle, gazing at the jagged tops of gravestones emerging through the soil, looking much like the crooked teeth encircling the gaping maw of a concealed predator.

It was another lurid vision, and he shook his head, wondering if recent events were taking that much of a toll on his meandering imagination.

Maybe they were.

Unsolved acts of destruction and viciousness, combining with the memory of one youth's violence years ago, the past and the present running along parallel pathways and moving directly towards the dark holiday. Halloween.

Well, the past wasn't about to repeat itself. Not if he could help it.

Cal trudged ahead, making for the small building which served as Ray's office and storage area. The elderly man was the only one who took care of the place, cutting the grass and trimming the overgrowth, and it was a lot of work, especially for someone of his age. Although he was reliable and out at the cemetery every day, it was clear that the grounds were too much for any single person to do on their own, but Ray was stubborn and the funds were limited, so that was it. Widowed many years ago, Ray had immersed himself in taking care of the cemetery by himself, and on more than one occasion had told Cal that this was where he belonged, close to the resting place of Rose, his beloved wife.

Who was he or anyone else to argue with the man's unwavering devotion?

The temperature was moderating, the afternoon moving along quickly. Cal wondered where the day had gone. Too many things on his desk, too many complaints, and not much help to be found. Well, he just had to deal with it. He was the town sheriff, and had spent his entire life in Shington, and knew that he would always live here. He loved it, and called it his home. Through his service, there was no greater compliment that he could give it.

Cal reached the building and grabbed for the handle. The door was unlocked. He walked in, calling out for Ray. There was no answer. He continued inside, looking around for the caretaker. The building was sectioned into two separate areas. The first consisted of a desk with files alongside it; a few shelves perched on the walls. Further back it grew rougher, the carpet giving way to concrete and opening up, the area filled with all the tools one could ask for in maintaining a cemetery or other large parcel of land. The back garage door was open, but there was no sign of Ray.

Exiting through the garage, Cal headed deeper into the cemetery, his eyes alert for the caretaker. Leaves tumbled about as the air kicked up, and the breeze felt good on his face. Careful not to step on any graves, he looked down at the headstones and the names and dates inscribed there, recognizing various family lines as well as a few individuals. He knew it was a sign of his own age and mortality, identifying with a growing number of those who had gone before him. Some who had been his friends.

*Grim thoughts, but he **was** in a cemetery, so what did he expect?*

Sliding mentally back to the reason for his visit, he wondered what had been the urgency in Ray's request. So far, nothing looked out of place. There was no damage to any of the markers, only the scars of weather and time, nicking and marring at the sturdy stone; a relentless assault of nature against man and his workings, and one in which the outcome was decisive and inevitable. The grass looked freshly cut, and Ray was obviously keeping up with his duties. The detective part of Cal was busy analyzing his surroundings, but no red flags stood out. He would just have to wait until he found the caretaker and see what had transpired.

Before too long the end of the cemetery reared up before him, a section which included some of the oldest gravestones in Shington. A huge oak tree sprawled there, a silent and gargantuan sentinel that simultaneously guarded against the hills and forests beyond, while retaining the boundaries of the old cemetery.

Looking up, Cal examined the woods in the distance, knowing that it was a no man's land with a few scattered home sites and thousands of acres of nothing but woodland and hills. Prime hunting grounds, and wild in their own right, it was a natural barrier protecting Shington from outside influences, and at the same time kept its residents contained within by a physically impressive landscape. It was beautiful country, and Cal both loved and admired it. But feared it? No.

For some reason then, he felt the slightest of chills, almost a primordial sense of wildness and chaos, realizing that he controlled the town within these perimeters, but the land past the borders was under its own governance. Clans of wayward families still inhabited these woods, obeying no law but their own protective instincts of close family and kin, which forbade the intrusion of anything which threatened their sovereignty.

Cal knew this for fact, having some experience running up against these folk. Once in while some of them rolled into town in a rusted pickup filled with family members, heading for the local market and hardware store for new supplies. They never bothered to hit the liquor store, as Cal knew they kept their own stills. Besides some odd stares from both sides, they were never any trouble during their treks into town.

Except for once…

He shook his head, remembering the incident, as well as the malefactor behind the trouble.

Nick.

The wayward youth had been up in the backwoods, causing mischief even there. *Damn, that had been reckless,* Cal thought. There was only one law in those hills, and it was in the defense of someone's family and property. If you stepped across that line, there was no one else to blame if you ended up missing, buried away somewhere in a shallow grave with a cold bullet hole in your head.

And that son of a bitch Nick had taken his personal brand of ugliness to the high places there and stirred things up.

Cal still had a clear image of Ramen Grable's weathered face as he strode with purpose into the police station on a cold October afternoon. The conversation had been brief but to the point. The town needed to rein in whoever was causing the problem, or there would be hell to pay.

And that was it.

Halloween had come and gone, and with it Nick. The problem had been eliminated, and the hill folk had returned to their cloak of obscurity. Cal had wondered many times what might have happened if things had become worse, and decided it was best not to...there were stories.

A bit puzzled, Cal looked in both directions, trying to figure out where the caretaker was. It would be uncharacteristic of the man if he'd left the cemetery in the daytime hours, and the sheriff knew his routine fairly well. Ray picked up needed supplies first thing in the morning and then came straight out to the cemetery for the day's work. Ray then worked until later afternoon or dusk, and retired to his small home, which was a short drive away, maybe a mile. That was about it. Reliable and honest, no one ever questioned the man's integrity. True, the workload was beyond any single person, but if the job became vacant, people wouldn't be lining up to fill it, especially considering the location. The place was on the fringe of town, and folk did have a slight superstitious streak running through their veins. Cal shrugged, but such was life in a small town.

Sighing, he lifted his head, staring into the hills, which had grown darker, the air clouding over. Storms were still in the area, although he had yet to feel a drop.

The Celebration

Now where was Ray? At that moment, Cal felt the first tingle of warning that something might have happened to the caretaker. There was mischief afoot in Shington, and someone was out there with a nasty penchant for violence and destruction.

Could it be worse than I thought?

It was possible, and for the first time that he could remember, he actually found himself feeling very uncomfortable out in the cemetery all alone, with the day growing late.

With that thought in mind, Cal was taken totally off-guard as something grabbed him by the shoulder. He pivoted backwards, ready for a confrontation. Gasping in surprise, he saw Ray's weathered face staring hard at him, and he eased up.

"Man, you scared the hell out of me. Please don't *ever* do that to one of my men, myself included." The sheriff shook his head in relief, but his expression turned grim at the look on the caretaker's face.

He had the look of the haunted in his eyes.

"I've seen him..."

"Him?" Cal asked. "Who? What are you talking about?"

Ray peered around, lowering his voice to a whisper, as if to conceal his words from unfriendly ears.

"Him. You know who I mean."

Cal was silent for a moment. The man was clearly spooked, there was no question. And he also smelled something. Alcohol.

"All right, back up there for a second here. Have you been drinking?"

"Yeah, but to hell with all that. I've seen him. Out here at dusk. I don't come out later than that anymore."

A growing feeling of dread began to crawl across
Cal's spine. Although the caretaker had yet to name
anyone, he already knew what would come next.

"Nick. I've seen him, Cal. And all the liquor in
the world won't make him go away. He's back."

The sheriff gazed intently at him, noticing
changes since their last meeting. Ray's hands trembled
ever so slightly. His eyes had dark smudges beneath
them, and his wrinkles appeared even more creased and
deeper than he remembered.

"Are you ill? Feel all right?"

"Don't give me that. I'm well enough, if it
weren't for that devil showing up lately. I've heard
about all the trouble. You think just because I'm old that
I don't know what goes on around here? Who do you
think is causing it all?"

"Not him, that's for damn sure. Someone is
trying to scare you. And the rest of us. That's all."

"If you had seen him you wouldn't be so quick to
laugh it off, sheriff."

Cal frowned. Ray never called him by his title.

"Relax for a minute. Humor me here, all right?
So tell me everything, Ray. What's been going on out
here? What about the vandalism?" Cal folded his arms,
but had the unpleasant sensation that they were being
watched.

The caretaker leaned closer, whispering as he
held up a pair of trembling fingers. "Two graves were
picked out. Marshall Raes, and Pete Swigler."

Cal knew them both. Marshall had been town
sheriff before him, suffering a heart attack not long after
retiring. And Pete? He'd owned a small garage and had
done all the police vehicular work. Why these two in

36

particular? Something was odd here. Was it a
coincidence that they had ties to Nick and his last fateful
venture? It was a disturbing connection, and showed a
more complex philosophy behind a few generalized
Halloween pranks.

It was troubling, to say the least.

Ray seemed to pick up on his apprehension.
"Something bad's in the air. You feel it too, don't you?"

Cal said nothing, nodding absently.

"Your gut is what you need to trust, sheriff.
Listen to it."

"Well, I need more than this to go on." Cal didn't
know where it was all leading, but he was trying to be as
neutral as possible in order to get the full truth from the
man.

The caretaker lowered his voice to a whisper
again. "I've seen him. A shadow stalking the edge of the
cemetery. Sometimes he seems to be part of the bushes
and trees, and then I see his outline, clear as day."

"How often do you see someone?" Cal was
careful not to agree with the man and bolster his claim.

"Nearly every night, since the first of the month.
If I stay and linger, that is. And it's getting late now."
He looked around, his eyes wide. "I'm leaving. If you
were smart you would do the same."

"Someone is trying to get under your skin, that's
all."

"Don't believe me then."

"I didn't say that…" Cal started.

"Well then see for yourself. *Be* a damn fool." Cal
was shocked at the bitterness in Ray's voice, something
entirely out of character for the man. The caretaker
turned and started walking away, and rather quickly,
considering his age.

"I guess you just need to see for yourself then, sheriff. Don't say I didn't warn you," Ray called back over his shoulder.

With that the man was gone, disappearing behind the massive tree, leaving Cal alone once more. It was as if the man had never been there. Reflecting on the bizarre conversation, Cal rolled around the various possibilities in his head. Here at least was a substantial lead connected to recent events. Most likely someone was doing their best to resurrect Nick's memory and cause damage to the town and its people. Several suspects came immediately to mind, but it involved putting together a good deal of speculation.

First to pop in Cal's head was Carson, who had been Nick's older brother. Part of this issue with Carson being involved was the fact that he'd left town even before his younger sibling's notoriety had begun to surface. No one had seen or heard from him in a very long time, but Carson had certainly been in trouble with the law along with his sibling. Last word was that he'd gone south, and that was about it. Cal had already placed a few calls, trying to locate his last whereabouts. It wasn't much, but it was a start at least.

Another suspect was Cass Andrews, Nick's old girlfriend. Unlike her problematic boyfriend, the girl had been associated with the events only through her relationship with him, and had never been found guilty of anything else…

…except for the *association* itself, and that might be just enough.

But Cal had a major problem thinking she would have anything to do with the vandalism. First of all, she had no prior record of breaking the law, however small. And she held a steady job, living at home with her mom, who was an alcoholic, although that was nothing new around town. Add that to the fact that she was a girl, and rarely would anyone but young males get into this kind of trouble. The notion was far-fetched, but Cal would look into the possibility, and probably within the next day or so. He hated to bother her, as she already carried a scourge of sorts from being close with the town's most famous villain.

But it was his job, and it had to be done. Very soon.

He lifted his head, gazing around at the graveyard and its surroundings. The sky appeared even darker yet, and it seemed some of the promised storm clouds had arrived. Dusk was nigh, and the cemetery had taken on a more menacing aspect now. Trees and headstones had transformed into half-legible silhouettes and outlines, as darkness eagerly encroached on this forlorn and quiet part of town. Cal didn't blame the caretaker for becoming spooked, but had the man gone over the edge that quickly since their last meeting, alcohol or not?

No. Most likely, Ray had become the victim of whoever was playing nasty tricks on the town. Adding to that was the fact that he'd been around during Nick's reign of fire, and he might be seen as an easy target.

Cal walked towards the middle of the graveyard, eyes scanning every possible hiding place. He felt the first drops of rain, and heard the wind whistling through hollow trees which were quickly losing their leaves. A brief flash of lightning arced through thick clouds overhead, and he listened to the low rumble of thunder in the distance. A growing sense of dread came over him, and he was angry for feeling such.

Grow up, he told himself. *You're the town sheriff, not some high school teenager.*

Or an old caretaker who had starting hitting the bottle while at work.

Regardless, the feeling of being watched grew stronger, enough so that he stopped, angling his head in several directions, trying to discover the source of his trepidation. He had good instincts, and tended to rely on them first.

Right now, they were blazing with warnings and red flags.

Cal pivoted, staring at the end of the cemetery which he'd just left behind, and in that same instant, a flash of lightning illuminated the grounds for the briefest of seconds. Then he *saw* it.

Directly in front of the huge oak tree a figure stood there, cloaked in a jacket blacker than the night. It looked like a young man staring at him, his face hidden in the shadows.

Cal stopped breathing, his heart pounding. Sweat trickled across his back, and then the lightning flickered out, the gloom taking hold once more. Whoever had been standing there was gone, and he pulled out his flashlight, scouring the area for the intruder. Shaken and confused, he took a few tentative steps forward, but there was nothing to be found. It seemed impossible that someone could have revealed themselves that quickly, and then ducked behind the tree and ran for the hillside.

Impossible...

The storm was closing and Cal knew that *something* had just happened here.

But who, or *what* had he seen?

The culprit behind the vandalism, or just a shadow of his own overworked imagination?

Undecided, he hurried away, knowing well that this was not the time or place to pursue the answer. He already knew that he would find nothing, and a small part of him hoped for that very outcome.

Cal jogged quickly through the graveyard back to his car, knowing that he would get very little rest that night.

An hour later Cal sat at the Shington Inn, drinking a beer and staring at the frosted mug as if it held the answers he was seeking. Outside, fat drops of rain pelted against the windows, the wind forcing tree branches to scratch against the side of the building.

All things considered, it had the makings of a night fit for neither man nor beast, as the saying went.

But was it fit for something else? A bold, mischievous prankster, or worse yet, perhaps an avenging ghost?

He wasn't prepared to believe that line of thinking. But that didn't mean his *imagination* was going to listen to logic.

Cal frowned, trying to bring himself out of this hole and shake himself clean. He was the town sheriff and that meant a ton of responsibility lay upon his shoulders, and he felt it all right now. This also meant that he couldn't fall into a panic mode, and latch onto the first explanation that came to mind, no matter how weird the circumstances. The town and its people were already superstitious. He simply couldn't join them in their predispositions. Not if he wanted to perform his office effectively.

Think, think, he told himself…

Yes, something strange had happened to him out at the cemetery that evening. Very weird, even terrifying. But it was his job to think things through, and come up with a variety of possibilities. Pursue them to the full extent of the law, and bring justice to the population. It was his calling, and despite his faults, he was true to this.

All right, settle down then, he told himself.

Cal sipped at his beer, looking around the room. The bartender, Roger, who also happened to be the owner, was leaning against a pole, watching the TV screen and chatting with Martin, one of the regulars. A scattering of other people half-filled the room, some in groups, while some drank alone, lost in their own thoughts. No one really paid him much notice. When he'd first walked in, several had greeted him, nodding his way or waving, but that was about it. They knew who he was, and what his office required. Some he called friends, others were not -- folks who had caused trouble before and ended up on the wrong side of the law. The Shington Inn wasn't a terrible place, but it had its seedier side, and if someone came here looking for trouble they could find it, sooner or later.

Jake was on patrol tonight, and Marlin was on first shift the next day. That left only himself and Josh Carpenter, the younger part-time officer on duty.

He lifted his head up, glancing around the bar. Roger had kept true to the season, decorating his place to the hilt. Paper skeletons dangled from the rafters, orange light strands were hanging from several spots, and spiders lurked in two corners, meshed in cobweb made from white yarn. Nestled alongside the jars of peanuts and pretzels sat containers filled with candy corn on the bar top. As if to further emphasize the approach of Halloween, someone had run a gamut of suitable tunes on the jukebox. *Monster Mash* had just ended, and now *Werewolves of London* was the choice selection, Cal listening to the catchy chorus with all the howling.

Maybe there's a werewolf loose in Shington, he thought. If not the Big Bad Wolf, then something just as nasty.

Shaking his head, he told himself that he needed to keep focused. Stick to the facts and analyze the evidence. Unfortunately, the evening's events had left a pretty strong impression on him, and like it or not, had spooked him in the process. It wasn't an easy feeling to just shrug off. He pictured the scene in the graveyard again, with the figure of the man silhouetted against the trees and illuminated by lightning.

What had he really seen out there? More importantly, who had he seen?

Storms, shadows, and darkness all had played a role in the episode. His senses could not be entirely trusted. But they also could not be ignored, as something tingled inside his brain, warning him that something was not quite right with the incident.

"Ah, hell," he muttered to himself, taking another swig from his glass. Cal felt like he needed a shot at the moment. Not that it would help anything, but it might make him feel a little better. Roger happened to be looking his way, and the sheriff nodded. The man came over seconds later, grinning.

"Cal, you look like you need a dose of something here. Am I right?"

"You know your trade all too well. A liquid medic all right."

"Of course I do. What else would explain my success and countless millions?"

"If that's true, you're a genius at keeping it hidden so well. Ah, it's been a tough night, and I'm thinking it wouldn't hurt for an extra kick in the rump. There's just so much going on lately. It hasn't been easy, you know."

"How about a shot of Jack? We all need to relax. I'll do one with you, and on the house, of course."

"Thanks. I can always count on you to cheer me up a bit." Cal smiled, appreciating the man's demeanor. Hell, he could sure use it right now.

Roger retreated to the bar and returned momentarily with a bottle. Looking around at his patrons once, he came over to Cal's table, sat down, and poured them both a shot.

"Cheers, sheriff."

They knocked their drinks back and inhaled them together, Cal enjoying the harsh liquid as it went down his throat and settled in his stomach. Yeah, he definitely had needed that...

"Ugly night out." Roger offered.

"No question there." Cal answered, wondering if his host might be able to help him out in other ways. "Hey, I want to ask you something."

"Sure. You're always welcome, you know. Hopefully there's nothing going on at my place that's causing you any concern." He raised an eyebrow in question.

"Nope, it's been quiet here. Don't worry."

"Great. That's the way I want to keep it too. So shoot. What's on your mind?"

"Thanks. It's good to be able to count on your friends."

True enough.

The Celebration

Cal continued. "All right. First off, has Ray been coming here lately?"

Without hesitation, Roger nodded. "Yeah, and dropping them pretty good. More than I can remember. Is there anything wrong with him?"

"I don't really know." Cal shrugged, not ready to give away too much. "Has he said anything to you about the cemetery?"

Roger frowned. "No. Just keeps to himself like usual."

Cal believed him. He knew he could trust Roger. Although there had been problems out of the Shington Inn in the past, it was mostly to blame on the drinking hole itself, and not the man who owned it. Roger had always cooperated when asked, and there was no doubt in Cal's mind that the man wanted no trouble at his place. It was bad for business, that simple.

"Here's another thing you might be able to help me out with. What have you been hearing from your regulars?"

"Such as?" Roger asked.

"Town gossip. The usual."

"Hmm. Well, it's a small town, and word travels fast, of course." Roger shrugged. Cal nodded.

The bartender continued. "And they talk about stuff. To me, each other. You know how it is. Everybody knows everyone else's business, whether people like it or not. Lately, there have been a lot of complaints about Halloween pranks going a little too far."

"Uh-huh." Cal drank from his mug. "This year they're way out of hand. We're working on it fulltime. But anything besides that. Anything really unusual?"

"Yeah. I would say so."

Now the sheriff's eyes perked up. He watched as Roger angled his head about, seeing if he was needed. The bar seemed hushed at that moment, hands gripping mugs, some of the patrons staring at the TV, and others just staring at nothing in particular. Cal looked at Roger, who had now lowered his head, along with his voice.

"Weird stuff."

He sipped from his own glass before continuing, the sheriff waiting patiently. "People been seeing things. Figures walking in the woods or along the cornfields, mostly at dusk or at night."

Cal felt electrified, his nerves tingling. "What are they seeing?"

Roger shook his head. "I don't know. Just some figure, someone wandering around, coming out of nowhere basically. I know, it sounds crazy, but that's what I've been hearing. And there's more. Noises coming from the woods, especially around the hills. The Bentley brothers were in here two nights ago and were out tracking. They told me something was following them down the trail going back to their truck. When they stopped, the noise stopped. Well, you know Blake. He can walk into a cave with a sleeping bear without so much as blink an eye. Cal, you should have seen his face. He was scared. There's more to their story, but he wouldn't talk any further, plus I didn't want to get him mad."

Cal listened, with more than a little trepidation moving through his own veins. He knew Blake well, and also his disposition. If Roger were telling the truth -- and there was no reason to believe otherwise -- then Blake might have encountered something similar to what he himself had just faced in the cemetery. Or worse.

The bartender leaned closer to him, his eyes narrowing. "There are some in town who are friends with those up yonder, the hill folk. Well, something has them spooked lately as well. And that can't be good."

Roger's statement caught the sheriff totally off guard. This was a complete surprise to him, and he felt his stomach do a quiet somersault. The *last* thing any of them needed was to have Ramen Grable and his people stirred up, looking for an outlet which would alleviate their anger. They were a renegade group, living by their own rules and laws, caring nothing for the consequences of their actions. If the mischief in town had trickled into the hills and high country, then things were a lot worse than he had thought. Worse and potentially dangerous.

Cal licked his lips, feeling the dryness on his skin. His mind raced in circles, trying to digest all the news and gossip.

"You all right? Cal?"

"Hmm? Yeah, I'm fine," he lied. "There's just a lot of stuff on my plate."

"I understand, believe me." Roger looked around, spotting a few thirsty glances spiking his way. "Well, let me take care of my customers. Drink to your heart's content. On the house, as usual."

"Thanks, I'll probably be leaving soon anyway."

"Suit yourself, sheriff."

With that, the bartender stood up and made his way across the room, grabbing a pair of mugs and heading back behind the bar. On the jukebox, Cal listened to *Spooky* being played, another seasonal favorite. Outside, the rain continued to hammer against the windowpane, and he was reluctant to go anywhere at the moment. Wouldn't it be great, he thought, if all his problems could be washed away by the unyielding rainfall? Carried off, and swept into the surrounding waterways to be lost forever. He felt comfortable there and felt as if he could lay down right on the floor. That would be a real kicker, he thought. The sheriff finally goes over the deep end. The town would have a field day…Well, looking back at what he'd seen earlier – or thought he'd seen – maybe he had already done just that.

But no. He was far from alone. People were alarmed and were also seeing strange things. He needed to plan out a well-defined course of action in order to find the source of all the trouble and discover what it really meant. And soon.

The Celebration was drawing closer with each passing day, and he was smart enough to realize the event and all the mischief were related somehow. Someone had a vendetta against the town of Shington and its people, and whether it was a bunch of spiteful teens, disgruntled citizens, or even a vengeful *spirit,* Cal was determined to get to the bottom of things.

With renewed vigor, he nodded to himself, polishing off the last of his drink. It was time to pay Cass a visit.

Fifteen minutes later the sheriff stood before the garage where Cass lived. Fully aware of the girl and her past (and present history), he stared down at the pair of jack-o-lanterns which gleamed at him through the mist and light rain. She'd been Nick's girlfriend, but had never been found guilty in any of his troubling affairs. She kept to herself. Her mother was a known alcoholic, shacking up with Clint, someone who caused enough problems on his own.

It was a pretty sad arrangement all around, he thought.

After all these years, he was still fairly sure that Cass had never matched up with anyone else after Nick's death, keeping quietly to herself and staying out of the town's watchful eye. True, she was innocent of those terrible events, but to many people it wasn't enough. She had been Nick's girlfriend, and that stigma would never be wiped away from her name. She might as well have had a scarlet letter hidden beneath her chest with a big *N* carved into it as neatly as the triangle eyes of a jack-o-lantern…

There was a light on inside, coming from the upper level, where she most likely had her bedroom. The two of them had very little interaction over the years, but Cal realized the girl felt no love for him or any of the others who served in the police department. Her feelings concerning the circumstances surrounding Nick's demise had been let known right away, and she had all but cursed the entire town and its people. After that, things had gone back to normal and Cass drifted into a self-imposed exile, living at home, working her job, and not doing much else. Little else was known about her, and she did a decent job keeping it that way. So in good conscience, there was nothing Cal could pin on her, at least for the moment. But it was hard to distance someone from a sordid past, and connections mattered. Considering the whole situation, there certainly existed reasons to suspect her as someone with the potential for involvement, if not directly, then maybe as an instigator behind someone else acting out the crimes.

Yes, it couldn't be ruled out.

Cal knocked twice, then backed away for a moment, feeling the raindrops splatter on his jacket. She had to be home, especially on a night as dismal as this. And if she wasn't, then that would draw his interest even more, for the girl would have little reason to be wandering town, having no social life or late working hours. It was a sad conclusion, but one which was backed up by facts, and ultimately that was the nature of his job.

He waited for a minute, and there was no response. The window shades were drawn closed, so he couldn't see anything inside. Pulling his coat tighter, he pursed his lips, and then knocked again, louder. The seconds moved along into at least another minute, and still nothing.

Well, she could be asleep.

He had no real idea of her personal habits, other than the fact that she rarely ventured from home if not for work, and that wasn't his normal business. However, if she was a suspect and he needed to gather information, then it *was* his business. Backing away, he glanced up to the second floor, trying to visualize the girl's face. He hadn't seen her lately, but he pictured her intense eyes and dark attire, like someone remaining in perpetual mourning. The common opinion was that the girl had never broken past her relationship and loss of Nick, and that was the biggest reason behind her mannerisms. Years later, she carried the event with her as if she had just left from his funeral.

The Celebration

Still gazing upwards, Cal was startled at a noise from somewhere behind him, and he pivoted quickly, his hand automatically moving to his weapon.

"Jumpy, sheriff?"

He stopped as he saw a figure standing before him cloaked in black against the rain. The long hair gave her away and he knew immediately that it was Cass. Cal narrowed his eyes, unhappy with being so easily startled, and for the second time that day. Any chance of surprise had obviously been shattered.

"Hello, Cass. How are you?"

The girl shrugged, one shoulder elevating slightly.

"I want to talk with you about some things, if you have a minute."

"Go ahead."

She offered nothing else, and Cal felt the tension between them. Like the townspeople, she also had never forgiven those who had been involved in Nick's death, and clearly held them to blame. And Cal had been one of the officers at the time…

"I'm sure you're aware of the vandalism taking place the past two weeks."

"I heard. How couldn't you in this place, where no one can keep their nose out of anyone else's affairs, and the main source of amusement is malicious gossip?"

Well, Cass had gone right to the point, leaving no doubt as to what her attitude was concerning Shington. Absolutely nothing had changed over the years. And it also gave the sheriff enough of a motive to place Cass in suspicion.

But was she this brazen as to cast herself as the prime suspect? That seemed incredibly arrogant and a bit far-fetched.

"Do you have any information which can help me find out who's responsible?"

"Are you accusing me of a crime, sheriff?" She laughed, but there was only sarcasm in the sound. "Pranks and tricks? Shouldn't you be looking for some young teenage boys instead of a harmless and respectable girl in her mid-twenties, who has never been found guilty of anything except being the girlfriend of the town's most notorious villain?"

"You still carry a lot of resentment about what happened. I can't change the way people feel about you, right or wrong. But from what I've seen, you haven't done anything to alter their perception for the better. Hiding from everyone isn't the answer."

"No, it's not. Getting out of here is the only way."

"Then why don't you leave? You're old enough."

The girl's head shifted downwards. "I guess because I still care about my mother, and don't want to see her end badly from that piece of garbage shacking up with her." Her eyes smoldered. "You want to find someone guilty of something? Start with Clint."

"What's he done? I do keep an eye on him, you know. He's no stranger to me. But if you know something that I don't…"

Her head rolled a bit, and Cal knew that he was touching on something the girl was uncomfortable with.

Well then…she did have her vulnerabilities after all.

"Nothing I can't handle on my own." Cal understood what it was now. "If he bothers you, I need to know about it. Listen, Cass. I know how you feel about me, and pretty much everyone else for that matter, but it's my job to protect the town and its people, despite your personal feelings. I won't hesitate to step in where I see trouble, hear me? If you think you can handle whatever's going on here, you might end up drastically wrong. Well?"

"I'll be fine."

She seemed unwilling to budge from her stance, and they matched gazes for a while, the rain continuing to fall on them.

"And I'm not accusing you of anything, but I need information from all sources. There are a lot of unpleasant coincidences with what happened before, and you can't possibly believe that your name isn't going to come up in some capacity. Now can you help me or not?"

And then, the ghost of a smile seemed to cross her face, but only briefly, so slight that Cal was uncertain if it had ever been there, and was perhaps only an illusion caused by the gloom and mist.

"Maybe it's Nick, come back from the grave."

The sheriff stared hard at her, at a loss as to whether she continued to bait him or if the girl was actually serious. "I'm trying to be helpful to you, and this is all I get? You can't live in the past forever, Cass. It's not healthy."

"It's my life to live."

"Spite and bitterness sure must be lonely companions. You could do so much better, you know. There are people around here who could be your friends, if you let them."

She tilted her head to the side, her thoughts unreadable.

"Well, I didn't come her to lecture you, although I doubt you'll believe me. If you feel as if there's something you can tell me, please come by the station or call me. And if there's anything that I can do to help you, don't hesitate."

Cass was silent. Frustrated at the girl's unrelenting demeanor, Cal tried one last time. "You know, I'm not judging you. But Nick did some terrible things to others. Vicious things. I have no idea what in the world you saw in him, but the only one to blame for what happened is Nick. He brought it on himself. Maybe he treated you like gold, but that doesn't erase all the destruction he left behind. And maybe, just once, you should think about the feelings and suffering of others instead of only yourself."

He waited for a response, but the girl turned her back to him, heading for the door. "Good night, sheriff." And that was the end of the discussion.

Sam Winston rummaged through the drawers in his desk, mumbling to himself as he pulled out a manila envelope. He'd only arrived back in town within the last hour, and wasn't planning on staying any longer than necessary.

"Hmm." He looked over the title page to his house, along with other real estate documents. "*These* I need…"

Gazing absently at the manuscript, he sat down at the small wooden table and poured himself a steaming cup of tea. Almost as an afterthought, he reached into the pocket of his suit jacket and pulled out a metal flask, dumping a shot of rum into the liquid. Things were moving quickly, and he was eager to put this part of his life behind him now. The town had served him well, and he liked to think it was a mutual arrangement, doing his best to uphold his end. The mayor had prospered nicely, and all the rumors were true -- that he was looking for property in Florida in the hopes of retiring there. He was ready for a change of scenery and an escape from small town politics and shortcomings. It was *his* time now, and there was no turning back.

Sighing, he moved about in the dimly lit kitchen. He was here under cover of night to avoid any prying eyes, and the last thing he wanted was to get tied up in the affairs of his office and delay what needed to be done. Jenn and the sheriff were more than capable of running things, and his phone calls took care of the rest. It's not that he was entirely shrugging off the duties of his office, but he certainly *was* doing his best to minimize his involvement. Besides, he would be back full-time by the Celebration, although it was going to be the last year he would be overseeing the cumbersome event.

Outside, it still rained, and he disliked the weather patterns of the north. Extremes of cold and hot in the winter and summer, with an occasional nice fall, but reliably wet springs. He looked forward to the consistent heat of Florida's environment. He was a firm believer that air conditioning was man's greatest invention.

Shuffling through drawers, he grabbed several things to snack on, mentally checking his list. He had no time to waste, and there was always a chance that someone would drive close enough to spot his Lincoln around back. His place was off the road a bit and he had a private lot, owning one of the largest homes in town. The front had a fairly long driveway which came up to the porch, where he normally parked. There was also a short dirt road in the back which merged into his rear tree line, and it was a convenient way for him to escape without the annoying stares of the main street citizens following all his movements.

Another twenty minutes or so and he would be off again. He walked into the dining room, bumping his knee on the rectangular table and cursing under his breath. That might leave a bruise. Rubbing the spot, his head snapped up as he heard a loud knock at the door.

"Damn. How can someone have seen me?" Irritated, he had no intention of answering. Instead, he worked his way to the front of the house until he reached the long, drawn curtains of the bay window, which looked out on the entire front yard. Carefully peering through a slit, he saw there was no car parked outside, and besides, he would have heard one pull up. He angled his head further, just enough so that he could make out the porch. Staring for a few moments, he was surprised at what he saw.

Nothing. Not a sign of anything or anyone.

He was certain that someone had knocked on the door, and loudly. Then where were they? It had been only a few seconds ago. He remained where he was, searching for movement. His porch light illuminated a wide enough area, although the weather helped deepen shadows and blended silhouettes. There was a line of bushes spreading to either side of the porch, but the shrubbery was not that deep or thick.

Could he have imagined the noise? No. Mistaken it for something else? Not likely. Still...

The mayor waited for at least two full minutes, then shook his head, backing off. He didn't want to delay his business any longer than possible, so he left the room, muttering to himself. When he reached the dining room, he stopped, his eyes narrowing as he heard the knocking again. It was *definitely* coming from the front door. Hurrying now, he ran back to the curtains, peering out and feeling more than a bit annoyed. For the second time he was caught by surprise, as the porch was again empty. But someone had just knocked. Could they have done so and then ran off, perhaps playing a prank on him? That now seemed the most plausible scenario. Halloween was nearly here, and the town certainly owned its share of tricksters. His hand rubbed absently across his chin, recalling the mischief that had been going on lately.

Yes, there just might be something connected here. He was the mayor after all, and a prime target if anyone was bold enough to tempt his wrath. If so, they played a dangerous game, and he would have no problem in calling the sheriff and his men to round up any troublemakers.

But he really didn't want it to go that far. All he wanted was to gather the things he needed and leave. That was all. Impatient though he was, the mayor also didn't relish the idea of wandering through his house with a bunch of teens lurking outside, their purpose unknown. It might be a harmless Halloween prank, and then it could be something more. Maybe they intended to break inside and burglarize his home. Then why knock on the front door? The answer was obvious and came to him immediately. It would be the safest way to see if he were really home or not. The direct approach.

What to do, what to do?

Seconds later his nerves got the better of him and he retreated, this time going upstairs into his bedroom. Opening the night stand, he pulled out the revolver he kept there for just this type of reason. It was a small town, but had its share of problems. Although he had always felt safe and secure within the town limits, there existed an element of crime and petty criminals. There were robberies and break-ins, just not a lot of them.

Making sure it was loaded, he now crept back downstairs, this time feeling a bit more confident, and angry. If someone broke in, he would not hesitate to defend himself. Standing in the dining room again, he worked his way to the front of the house, stopping in mid-stride as a loud knock rang out, but this time it came from the window to the right, only a few feet from where he now stood. Genuinely startled, he snapped his head over, staring at the drawn curtain. He was glad that it was closed, or else he might have been face-to-face with his stalker. He didn't want to lose the element of surprise. That much was certain. Carefully he moved forward, steering away from the middle, instead trying to sneak a glimpse from the side, where he might finally catch a peek at his tormentor, and maybe give *them* a shock of their own as they stared down the barrel of his pistol. Hardly daring to breathe, he looked outside, expecting to see a sinister face pressed in close against the window.

But again he saw nothing. It was dark, but there was just enough light for him to have seen someone standing there.

Gritting his teeth, the mayor was growing tired of the game, but he wasn't quite done yet. The gun bolstered his courage, of course, and he knew he held the advantage. He wasn't ready to believe the hidden intruders were armed and dangerous. Not yet at least.

He waited there for a minute.

Then another.

All remained quiet, the only sounds the tick-tock from the grandfather clock in the main room and the soft patter of rain licking against glass.

Florida couldn't come soon enough for him. This was ridiculous. When he caught the culprits, they would pay dearly, prank or not. He felt his stomach growl. Part hunger, part nerves, he knew. He was also starting to sweat -- a combination of anxiety plus being overweight.

Without warning, the front door shuddered, as if something heavy had crashed right into it.

"Bastards..." He was furious now, and a bit scared, but his anger won him over as he hurried to the door, ready to confront his tormentor. It was game time.

Boom!

Another crash against the door. *What the hell were they doing out there? Trying to knock it down?* He went a few steps further.

Boom!

The noise was so loud that he found it unbelievable that the door could remain standing. It was as if a huge crane had rammed against the frame. He went another few feet, going slower.

Boom!

This time he could actually see the door vibrate from the power being waged against it. No one could be that strong. It had to be half a dozen men out there trying with all their might to break it down, all of them slamming their bodies and fists into the wood in madness, determined to destroy the panel and break inside. It made no sense, but the mayor had no time to think, as he now stood directly before it. Breathing heavily, he weighed his options. He was tempted to fire a shot right into the door and scatter his attackers away, although that would run the risk of seriously injuring someone, even possibly killing them.

Still…

He didn't know who was out there and how dangerous they were, but based on their aggressive action, he would be within his rights to protect himself, although he didn't want to kill someone in the process. That would be sure to complicate his situation here, and with him so close to leaving it all behind. He had to be careful…

Boom!

Something outside thundered against the door, and the rest of his patience melted away.

"Son of *bitches*…"

Pistol held high before him, he turned the bolt and hurled the door open, finger on the trigger. Mouth open wide and screaming in rage, the mayor pressed forward in fury only to find…

…nothing.

The porch was empty. No one stood there, nothing moved.

Impossible.

Absolutely impossible. No one could have moved away that quickly without him seeing their retreat.

He blinked, trying to understand what was going on here, but for the life of him he had no answer. He then examined the outside of the door, and found it to be smooth and unmarked, appearing almost new in the gloomy lighting.

"Impossible." He whispered the word to himself again, no other thought or explanation coming to him. Just that single *word*, and one that meant both everything and nothing to him at that point in time.

The Celebration

His eyes scanned the front yard, and everything appeared normal. Nothing stirred, and even the rain had now stopped, almost as if it had been a willing accomplice trying to obscure his vision and ability of perception. He was shocked to see the grass and porch abandoned, not a trace of anything living to be seen. But the revelation that there was nothing out there was more than he could stand. The silence and emptiness of that lonely sight was worse than the alternative of facing down any intruders. He would have felt more at ease if he now found himself confronting a mob of youths all staring at him, challenging him with their arrogance.

Anything but *this*... the emptiness. The silence.

His only companion was the night, with all the hidden secrets it held within its shadowy cloak. His imagination was a live creature inside of him, stoking the fires of possibility and giving birth to the seeds of deep-rooted terror.

"It doesn't make any sense." He whispered to himself, alarmed by how loud his voice sounded against the forsaken backdrop of his once familiar front area, now transformed into a haven of unknown things. His hands trembled.

He couldn't stand there any longer trying to figure things out. He was too vulnerable, too exposed. And despite seeing nothing at all out there -- no explanation for whatever had been responsible for making the terrible pounding against his door -- he felt like he was being observed.

The sensation came over him all at once, washing over him in one frightening revelation. Something was watching him, and the very thought of it immobilized him for several seconds, until he at last wrenched himself free from the terror and slammed the door behind him. He leaned heavily against it, feeling the cold, clammy sweat coating his back. His breathing was harsh, and he felt an unpleasant tightness in his chest. Hoping that it wasn't his heart, he masked his face with one hand, lowering the barrel of his gun. With some effort, he pushed himself away, locking up, knowing that he had no choice now but to call for help. Something very strange was going on here, and he couldn't face it alone.

In the same moment as he moved away, the door behind him shuddered as a tremendous force smashed against it, so hard that he felt the vibrations in the wood flooring at his feet. He stumbled forward, falling to the floor and landing hard on his stomach, knocking the air from his lungs. Again the door shook, and he crawled away, deeper into the house, his horror reaching a new level.

How could this be happening? Nothing had been out there a second ago. Nothing! Was he going mad?

If so, he would rather embrace the thought of losing his mind than consider the alternative – that something utterly unknown was responsible for what was going on here. Something strange, and dangerous.

The mayor gained his feet, huffing his way into the kitchen, bumping into a chair in his panic. He grabbed the phone off the receiver and pushed the first code which dialed directly into the police office. Cal or some of his men would be out here in a few minutes. All they had to do was pick up... *Boom!*

This time it was the kitchen door that was under assault. Only a few feet from where he now stood, the mayor quaked with fear, looking at the open space between the blind where the attacker had to be. Eyes gaping wide, he tried to make out an outline, or at the very least the silhouette of who was out there.

The Celebration

Instead he saw nothing. No shape, no movement, not a hint of anything but the night and shadows.

In that instant he lost it for a moment, the impossibility of his situation striking him down. His mind swirled and things went blank. When he finally opened his eyes, he found himself kneeling on the floor, awareness coming to him with a fury, his only thought being *nightmare.*

He looked around, remembering everything, realizing that he had blacked out only briefly. And then he saw something which terrified him to the bone…

The kitchen door was partly open, the wind gently moving it.

Open?

The intruder had broken the lock, and now nothing separated him from who – or what – was out there. How long had he been out? It couldn't have been more than a few moments. But long enough. Were they out there waiting on the back porch? Or worse yet -- and the very thought made him sick to the stomach – were they now in the *house*?

He had to act quickly. He was sure that his life depended on it. He clenched his hand but found that the gun was missing. Had he dropped it? Or had it been taken from his grasp while he swooned? Remembering the phone then, he picked up the receiver which dangled only inches above the tile floor. He punched in the code, waited a few seconds, but heard nothing. The line was dead.

The mayor's chest felt like it was in a vice, and he knew that the stress was taking its toll on his heart. He'd never had problems before, but that didn't mean he wouldn't now. He got to his feet and stumbled into the dining room, heading for the stairs. Safe or not, it seemed a much better decision for him to stay in the house than venture outside into the darkness. Maybe he would have the opportunity to make a break for his car. Hurrying ahead, he rummaged in his pocket, slightly reassured as he felt the keys still in there. Sweating profusely, he gained the second floor, sprinting down the hall toward his bedroom.

Please, let it be empty. Please.

Weaponless and with no help on the way, he had little recourse than to lock himself in the bedroom and hope his tormentor went away. There was no relief in the notion at all, but he had nothing else left. The mayor paused before the door, which was open. He always left it open, although that meant nothing. With great trepidation, he poked his head inside, but it appeared empty.

So had the front yard. And the kitchen door. Empty...

There was nothing for him to do but to go in. He flicked on the light switch, gave another look, and then slammed the door behind him. Immediately he went to the bed, pushing it before the door, attempting to bolster his defense. What else could he use? The dresser was next, and soon he had the bulky furniture blocking the entrance as well. Moments later he collapsed into a large wooden chair which sat before his desk. The house was quiet, and he suddenly realized that there was more than one way into the room. He went over to the window, and although it was locked, that fact gave him little comfort. There was no way to gain access unless someone had a ladder or could climb a sheer wall of brick. Regardless, he turned his desk on its side and then blocked it against the window, sealing it off. Satisfied, he again sat down, and waited to see what would happen next.

He didn't have to wait very long.

Something powerful crashed against the bedroom door, causing the panel to shudder violently.

"Go away!" He screamed. "Or I'll shoot!"

Without his weapon it was nothing more than a bluff, and it proved to be ineffective, as the door shook again.

Boom!

The mayor huddled there, helpless to do anything except watch and listen, as time and again the door was assaulted by some unseen force from the hallway, relentlessly pounding against it.

"What do you want from me?" His voice shook badly and was little more than a whimper. "Go away, please…"

Boom!

Pieces of the door broke away and the objects blocking it pushed inwards.

Inching toward him…

The mayor shrunk into himself, all possible explanations falling flat. There had been no one outside. Not in the yard. Not on the porch. He'd seen nothing at the kitchen door. *No one…*

And yet something was coming after him, powerful and invisible. There had to be some trick being played here. Something which had him completely fooled. Someone had gone to great lengths in order to frighten him.

And it was working.

The feeling of tightness in his chest was proof enough. If this continued much longer, he might very well be frightened to death. With no weapon at his disposal and no help forthcoming, the mayor was at the mercy of his unseen attacker.

"I'm not a bad man. I've done nothing wrong," he whispered.

At this, the pounding stopped, and he could have sworn that he heard faint laughter from somewhere in the hallway, the sound chilling and terrible.

But he wasn't sure. He could be certain of nothing at this point in time. Maybe he was completely mad by now, and all of this was in his head.

But then the door splintered into fragments, the bed, desk and dresser sliding slowly across the floor.

Too scared to move – or no less stand and defend himself -- Mayor Sam Winston stared with unblinking eyes, searching for movement. Could he plead with them for mercy, promise to do them a favor, anything? It seemed he would finally have a chance to confront his attacker, and maybe understand what was going on. And why.

The floorboards creaked as someone approached.

But still he saw nothing.

He again had the feeling of being watched, although the intruder was still cloaked somehow, either in shadow or by some other means.

"What do you want?" he croaked. "Where are you? Please tell me."

And then, before his disbelieving eyes, a silhouette appeared in front of him, all shadows and haze. He covered his face, cowering into a corner, and he knew that he would never see Florida again as something strong threw him up against the wall and darkness took him.

The Celebration

"Well, Clinty-*boy*! Still hanging around your favorite watering hole, I see."

Taken by complete surprise, Clint went flying through the air, crashing against a pair of metal trash cans and falling in a heap. Stunned by the attack, he peered through the twilight, making out a tall figure, and recognizing the voice.

It was Jake Saddle.

Clint tasted blood in his mouth, and maybe a broken tooth as well. Before he had time to examine himself further, Jake was already on top of him, grabbing his jacket and pulling him roughly to his feet. Even if Jake hadn't been an officer of the law, Clint would never have stood a chance against the bigger and stronger man, and both of them knew it very well.

"What do you want? I didn't do anything…"

His sentence ended abruptly, as he was flung mercilessly against the wall, the air knocked from his lungs. He would be lucky to walk away without any cracked ribs.

"No, you never do anything wrong, do you, Clinty-boy? One of our town's leading citizens. Why you're pretty much a stand-up guy in Shington. Hell, maybe you'll be voted into office one of these days."

Jake pinned him against the wall, Clint not even daring to resist. This game had been played before, and the only thing Clint could hope for was that he could offer Jake whatever it was he wanted. If not…things would get a lot uglier. "I see you been shacking up with Katy Andrews. Why in the world she wants to keep your worthless hide around I'll never understand. Of course, she hits that bottle pretty good too, so I guess you two have something in common." Clint was silent.

"Not very talkative tonight, huh? That might change soon."

"Wait, man. What do you want from me?"

Jake brought one knee up, slamming Clint in the stomach, then watched him slump to the ground.

"You know, even in school I knew you would never amount to anything. All those times I kicked your ass didn't make you any smarter or tougher. You should have just left town and moved on. But here you are, and here I am."

Clint stared up at him, biting back an angry retort. Jake was baiting him, looking for any reason to work him over further.

"Now listen to me, Clint. I can make life a hell of a lot more miserable for you than getting thrown around a little. Right?"

Clint nodded. "I'm listening."

Jake folded his arms. "There's a lot of bad stuff going down lately. Don't pretend you haven't heard any of it."

Clint shook his head. "I've heard, but I had nothing to do with it."

"I believe you. You would never do anything so obvious." Jake sneered at him, but the other man said nothing. "Do you know anything about who's behind it all?"

"I swear I don't know anything. I have no idea who's doing it. Probably a bunch of kids." "Maybe, maybe not. But I'm going to find out. And Cal wants answers, and an end to all this crap real soon. Before the Celebration. We want someone locked up. Put behind bars where they belong."

"If I hear anything you have my word, I'll let you know right away."

The Celebration

Jake made a sound in mockery. "Your word means nothing to me. If you weren't so afraid of me you would never come through."

"I don't want no trouble with you, Jake. You know that."

"I don't know anything about what goes on in that twisted little mind of yours, Clint."

Frowning, Clint asked again. "What do you want from me?"

Leaning close, Jake smiled, but there was nothing but nastiness in the expression. "You *can* help me after all." He pointed a finger in Clint's face. He then straightened, staring down at the other man for a moment.

"It's about Cass."

Clint never blinked, wondering if the girl had said something after all about his advances.

"First of all, I want you to back off from her. If I so much as catch a whisper that you're trying to make her, you're dead. You'll be buried up in the hills where no one can ever find you. Do I make myself clear?"

"Yeah," Clint answered, unsure of what was going on here.

Jake looked down at him for a few seconds. "All right. Here's the tricky part where you come in. I want you to watch her like a hawk, without being obvious. Find out if she's doing anything unusual, talking to people, going anywhere that seems odd."

"Do you think she's the one doing all the stuff?" "Listen up, Clint. You're not to do any thinking on your own, you hear me?" He grabbed Clint's jacket again, shaking him hard.

"All right, yeah, yeah…" "Just do what the hell I want without questions. And you tell this to no one.

If word gets out about our little conversation…" His voice trailed off.

"I swear I won't, Jake."

"So you keep an eye on her, and I'll check back with you. In three days I'll meet you out here again. If you find anything which might be useful, then come down to the station and leave me a message. Understand?"

"Yeah, no problem."

"And if I need to find you before then, I know where you're at. Now get out of here, and remember everything we talked about. Do what I tell you, and maybe I'll leave you alone. Maybe…"

With that Jake turned and walked away, never looking back. Jake peered around the corner before walking out from behind the back of the bar. Satisfied that no one had witnessed the confrontation behind the building, he made his way back to his vehicle.

Cal sat at his desk, glancing down at the calendar. It was hard to believe that Halloween was only a few days away, and with it the Celebration, and they still hadn't found out who was responsible for all the vandalism and maliciousness. Five minutes ago he'd received a phone call concerning the whereabouts of Carson James. It seemed Nick's older brother was now serving a prison sentence in a small town near the Mexican border. His situation didn't come as much of a surprise to Cal, knowing his past. It was a bigger surprise that he was even alive anymore, and not underground in some unmarked grave, with either a plastic bag over his face or his body riddled with bullet holes. Regardless, it took him off the potential suspect list.

There were other names on that list, of course. A few high school kids who were in trouble from time to time. Johnny Sepal, a dropout who was no stranger to the town jail. And Cass as well, who Jake was keeping an eye on.

But as of yet, all of them had either strong alibis or hadn't done anything suspicious as of late. So he remained stumped, while the pranks continued. Some of them minor, others more disturbing.

And where the hell was Sam?

The mayor should have been back by now. The phone calls to Florida failed to reach him. He had left the state a few days ago and was supposed to be headed back north. Maybe he was tied up with some financial issues. Maybe he'd made an unexpected side trip somewhere else on a whim or even an emergency. Nothing else was known as to where the man could be reached. All this added up to a growing pile of paperwork and phone calls directed to the sheriff's office, along with all the complaints. He simply couldn't get ahead, and especially not until the culprits were found and locked up. It would be great if this were to occur prior to Halloween, but he had a growing sense of dread that it wasn't to be, and something was going to happen during the Celebration, something bad. He could feel it in his bones.

Just like it had seven years ago when Nick was still around...

Cal was convinced more than ever that these were related events, whether by someone with an axe to grind, or some punk following in Nick's notorious footsteps. Either way, there was someone walking the streets of Shington who had a very nasty streak inside of them. It was unknown just how far they were willing to go to get their point across.

It was a disturbing thought, and little wonder that he'd been so edgy lately. Thinking was a big part of his job, but he had a slew of things to do and couldn't afford the luxury of sitting at his desk all day. It was early afternoon and time to get out of the office. He now had Marlin and Josh splitting twelve hour shifts on patrol, the younger officer also working full time, at least until they caught the culprit behind the vandalism and other random acts of mischief, so that freed Jake and himself to focus entirely on the case, no matter how long it took. He just hoped that Jake wouldn't go overboard getting there. The deputy could be a loose cannon at times, and it worried Cal. He'd been an officer nearly as long as himself, serving at the time Nick had been around.

Standing up and finishing the last of his coffee, Cal grabbed what he needed and left the room, pausing to chat with Arlene for a moment.

"I'll be out for a while, so I don't expect to see you tonight." "Are you heading over to the town square?" Arlene asked.

"Yeah. I'll check out the tents. See if the boys over at the fire company are satisfied. Wouldn't want to have the Celebration go up in smoke."

Arlene raised her eyebrows, as if wondering as to how serious the sheriff was by his statement.

"See ya tomorrow, Arlene."

"Good evening, sheriff."

"And Arlene, if you happen to hear back from the mayor, tell him to call me at home later."

"I will."

The Celebration

With that Cal headed out the back door, locking it behind him. He opened the door to his car and was off in a minute, mind swirling around all the things on his agenda. Heading down Main Street, a few blocks later he entered the town square where he double-parked in front of a large tent which was surrounded by several smaller ones.

They were setting up for the Celebration.

People milled around, and he recognized everyone, some smiling and nodding in his direction. Immediately a man in a white coat approached him. It was Glen, the town coroner. He was small, in his late fifties, nearly bald, with mouse-like eyes. Cal hated to admit it, but the man's appearance was a perfect fit for his occupation.

"Evening, Glen."

"Sheriff, I need to talk with you." Normally, they were on a first name basis. But something was odd about the man's greeting, and now that he focused on him, Glen looked more haggard than usual.

"I'm here. What can I do for you?"

Glen looked around, then turned back towards Cal. "I'm scared."

"What's the matter?" Already Cal felt a chill go down his spine. This was the last thing he needed to hear. From anyone.

"Last night at my office." It was Glen's work place, which served him in every needed capacity for the nature of his job. It was about a mile to the north, and the sheriff was of course no stranger to the small building.

"Yeah? Go on."

"Well, I heard a knocking at my door. Right after dusk. I was doing some paperwork, getting ready to pack up for the night. I went to check and there was no one there."

Cal nodded slightly.

"I went back inside and I heard someone knock again. This time I went to the window, but saw nothing. Nobody was out there."

"Kids maybe? Halloween is almost here, and there's been a lot of pranks going on lately, which I'm sure you've heard about."

"I have. And you know how I feel about all that nonsense."

The sheriff said nothing, letting the man get his story out. "I was getting angry now, but I figured the same. Damn kids. Well, I went back again, and there was a knocking, for a third time. Louder now, like someone was either furious, or wanted to make me scared. So I went to the phone, thinking I was going to get one of your officers over here and take care of whoever was out there, but the line was dead. Nothing. And all this time the knocking continued. I really didn't know what to do, but I hurried to the window and peeked out. As soon as I looked through the blinds, the noise stopped. Just like that."

"And did you see someone?" Cal asked.

The coroner shook his head, his eyes wide. "It gets worse. I stayed there for a minute, and then another. And suddenly the knocking started again, but there was no one out there! Nobody. It was too much, so I ran back inside and straight out the back door. Luckily Milton was there, getting ready to get in his car. I told him about what happened, and we both got in and drove to the front. There was no one on the sidewalk, and nothing looked unusual."

The Celebration

"You saw nothing? Kids or anyone else further down the block?"

"No. I had Milton drive me home. I was pretty shaken, and he let me stay over for the night. He came in with me this morning. I didn't want to call you last night, figured you were home. But I wanted to see you today, and knew you were coming over here. I don't know what to make of it all but I'm worried, with all the talk around town. I've been carrying my gun with me. And I won't hesitate to use it, sheriff."

There was an intense look in his eyes, one that Cal had never seen there before. Was there more to the story? He pressed the man further.

"Do you have any idea who it might be, or is there someone who has reason to be angry at you?" It was an aggressive statement, putting the coroner on the defensive. "How would I know? Probably just a bunch of kids with nothing better to do.
And it's your job to keep people safe, sheriff, or do I have to remind you?"

Cal's face was expressionless, trying to read into the man's words. He was obviously scared, but Cal thought there was something else he was leaving out. He couldn't put his finger on what, or why, but his instincts told him that the whole story wasn't being told here.

"No, you *don't* have to remind me. But you also know how small our force is. I have everyone working full time, with Jake and me investigating all the trouble. Plus with Sam still out of town and not returning phone calls, I'm picking up all his work. I could use some more help these days. We're doing our best. And I would be real careful of pulling a trigger on anyone, especially if it turns out to be some wiseass kid."

Glen's face clearly showed that he wasn't satisfied with the answer. "A lot of people are talking around town."

"Yeah? And what's that supposed to mean? Why don't you tell me, Glen?"

The coroner fidgeted. His bark was worse than his bite, Cal knew. And he also knew how unpopular the man was. Unlikable, and sometimes downright rude, he walked around with his office on his chest as if he demanded the highest respect possible.

"Maybe you're not doing *enough* is what some people are saying."

It wasn't news to Cal, but he refused to let Glen – or anyone else – get to him. So far their leads had turned up nothing. Between himself and Jake, they were putting in very long hours, practically living out of the station the past few days.

Cal pointed a finger at the coroner. "Listen, I'm hardly home anymore. If someone wants to come over and apply for my job, let them go ahead. Why don't you do it yourself? I think you'll find it a lot harder than sitting around waiting for a dead body to plop down on your desk. Now if you'd let me go, I need to get back to work. Besides looking for criminals to lock up, a pile of red tape on my desk from Sam's office, and a hundred phone calls a day, I also have to make sure things like the Celebration are going smoothly and the place doesn't go down in flames. I'll have my guys keep an eye on your office. Now if you'll excuse me, I need to go."

He brushed past Glen's small figure, the coroner's eyes smoldering with anger. Cal had never liked the guy to begin with. He was secretive, and only looked out for himself, whether it was business or personal. He realized he had been harsh with him, but he was getting tired of trying to solve all the town's problems as of late. Not only as the head of law enforcement, but now as town administrator. It was basically a given that Sam was going to leave soon, most likely after the New Year. There was no other candidate for his office that Cal knew of, and *he* didn't want it either. And the more he took on the temporary duties of acting mayor, the more people would expect from him.

Shaking his head, he walked over to the tents, focusing on his job now and trying to see if there were any safety issues. He inspected the outlets and wiring, looked over the poles and fixtures, all the time jotting down notes. He found several potential problems, and after fifteen minutes of doing his walkthrough, he hunted down Jackson Frey, who was supervising the setup. Cal didn't want to stay there any longer than possible, so he gave the man his report and told him he would be back tomorrow to make sure his orders had been followed. Shortly, he was in his cruiser again, feeling the need for a good cup of coffee.

Now it was on to his next stop, and one that might not necessarily go very well.

He continued driving for a while, heading to the north of town and into even more rural areas. Pulling up to a dirt driveway, he paused for a moment, looking up an incline which wound its way between fields of grass which soon gave way to the forest that surrounded the valley, the land rising higher into the foothills. Several hundred yards in the distance lay a small farm, home to the Bentley brothers. Roger had mentioned that the two men had encountered something strange a few days ago, and Cal had little doubt that it was related to the rest of the unexplained events taking place around Shington. He needed to follow any lead which materialized, even if it meant questioning some of the seedier members of the community.

The Bentley brothers happened to fit that description perfectly. Known poachers, they kept to themselves for the most part, and no one dared trespass on their property. Cal knew they kept a still in the nearby woods, and he also knew they were close to Ramen Grable and his kin, probably related. He needed to step carefully here, but without being intimidated. He wasn't afraid of the men, but there was a real risk of increasing the fragile tension. On the outskirts of town, the law was in effect only when he and his men were present. Proving that any laws had been broken was never an easy thing to do in these hills.

The sheriff pulled his cruiser into the driveway, tires crunching over stone and dirt. The leaves were in brilliant color now, and fall was certainly in full display. It took him a full minute until he reached the house. He heard a loud barking as dogs alerted the property owners of their unexpected guest. Cal left his vehicle, wary of any stray animals, but there were none in sight. Almost immediately the front door opened and out stepped Blake Bentley, his face masked. Cal leaned against his car, motioning the man towards him. Blake rubbed a hand across his chin and with long strides came forward. He was meaty and tall, a few inches over six feet, wearing a rust colored flannel shirt. There was no sign of his older brother anywhere.

"Hi Blake."

The man said nothing, frowning instead. After several seconds, he spoke. "What do you want, sheriff? You got no business here that I know of."

"It's my business to go where my job demands. I don't see how that's too hard to understand." He moved off from the car, refusing to let the man intimidate him.

Blake stopped only a few feet from him, staring him down, but Cal didn't flinch.

"Don't try and give me any trouble, Blake. I'm really not in the mood today for any crap." He said it without blinking an eye. "Despite your guilty conscience, I'm not out here to harass you. Are we clear?"

Blake scowled at him, looking back towards the house for a moment as if considering his options. "I'm here to ask you and Terry some questions. I'm looking for help." He opened his hands in a gesture of appeal, hoping to soften the man's demeanor. "All right?"

"Help from us? What's this all about?" "There's a lot of trouble going around lately. It seems to have affected every part of town. Someone is going out of their way to make life miserable for everyone in Shington. I want to catch the bastard and lock him away."

A strange look crossed Blake's face, quickly passing, but it was too late. Cal knew something had spooked the man pretty badly.

"You know something? Or you've seen something yourself? Well?"

But Blake didn't look like he was willing to concede anything. Cal, gambling, decided to throw something in as a bargaining chip.

"Listen, Blake. If you help me out here, maybe I'll forget about that still you have up there." Cal pointed to the woods directly behind the house. "No use denying it. I know all about it, and I can tear it apart piece by piece any time I feel like it. Don't think I can't, or won't."

Blake appeared ready to shout, his face brightening.

"Just hold on a second, here," Cal said raising one hand in the air for emphasis. "I'm willing to ignore what's back there for now. I could really use your help. Maybe we can come to some understanding between us. It wouldn't hurt to try, you know."

The other man bit his lip for a second, then nodded. "All right, sheriff. I'll give it a shot. Let's go inside."

"Will do. After you."

Cal followed after him, the pair going up a few steps onto the wooden porch, the planks creaking beneath their boots. Blake opened the screen door and Cal came behind. The living area was surprisingly clean and organized, with a brick fireplace dominating the room. A chocolate Lab mix lifted its head, sniffing the air.

"Don't mind Agnes. She has a bad hip. Have a seat."

Cal nodded, sitting down on a wood futon which was covered by a thick blanket. "Drink?" Blake asked.

"Coffee would be nice. Don't spike it with anything though."

Blake stopped in midstride.

"Just kidding. Kind of…but I really don't want any of that homemade whisky in it. Wouldn't want my stomach pumped to get a hold of any possible evidence."

The man paused as if considering the remark, then finally grunted, moving away. Cal figured he got the joke. He hoped to break the ice with the brothers. There really hadn't been any incidents for a while, even though he always kept an eye on them. He could live with some of the town residents making their own liquor, as long as it didn't turn up at any underage drinking parties. And poaching was not exactly unheard of, although he would still bust anyone caught shooting game out of season.

"Sugar or milk?" Blake yelled in from the kitchen.

"Neither. Black as night."

A minute later the man reappeared, carrying two mugs. Setting one down before the sheriff, he seated himself on the sofa opposite from where Cal sat. Neither man said anything for several long moments, each sipping his drink.

Putting his cup down, Cal opened the conversation. He was busy, and had little time to dance around the purpose of his coming there. "All right, Blake. I meant what I said before. There's a lot of trouble going on lately. And no, I'm not accusing you or your brother at all. I have no reason to. But I'm trying to gather as much information as possible. I need to hear anything you can tell me. We're looking for all the leads we can get, and my guys are working around the clock. And since you have some ears to the outer parts of the country, I figured I would touch base."

Blake nodded, but was silent. Cal watched his face carefully, and he was convinced that the man had either experienced something himself or had knowledge about it. He could see it in Blake's eyes.

"I think you know something, don't you?" Cal pressed him for answers.

Blake stared into his mug for a while, then responded. "I don't think there's anything I can tell you that can help."

"Try me. I'm listening."

"Hmm." He shook his head, looking into the kitchen for a moment. "Here it is. But I warned you…Terry and me been finding some of our animals missing the other week. A couple hens and stuff. We did our usual thing, trying to find out what was responsible. Fox, probably. Maybe a hawk."

"Yeah?"

"Nothing in our traps, although you can't get a fox anyway. Too damn smart. No tracks. So we went out at night and waited. Just the dogs freakin' out, but we never saw anything. Then it stopped. So a few days ago we went out, up above."

He pointed to the back of the house, and Cal knew that he was referring to the surrounding woods and foothills.

"Coming back at dusk, it was almost dark, and we were at the Point. You know where I mean, right?"

Cal nodded. The Point was a barren piece of rock which looked down on the valley. There was a slide below it, and there it opened, giving up one of the most spectacular sights in the area.

"We heard a noise ahead, like a howling or something. Strange, but it wasn't anything we recognized. So moving slow, we got near the big rock, and then we heard another sound, like someone was…well, laughing at us."

Cal listened close, feeling the same sense of strangeness that he had experienced himself the other night.

"Terry yelled out, trying to recognize who it was. We were thinking it was one of Ramen's boys, but they didn't say anything back. And we just heard the laughing. We looked at each other, wondering who might be messin' with us. It was getting late, but we know these hills like the back of our hand. Something moved then, real quick. We both caught a glimpse of someone moving through the woods, more like a shadow than anything else."

"You couldn't make out any details?" Cal was almost afraid to hear Blake's response.

"Nope. Too dark. We followed after, knowing that we were a few dozen yards to the Point. Well, we got up there, and you know it opens up and you're right at the cliff. But the weirdest thing is, no one was there." Cal was confused by Blake's story, and if he hadn't seen something so weird himself, he would have written it off to bad liquor and dim lighting. But he *had* seen something – and heard enough – than to simply shrug it away, and that made all the difference.

"All right. So what did you do next?" "We hurried over, my brother swearing the whole time. Someone had to be pretty damn quick – and smart – to lose us without being seen. It didn't make any sense."

"And the ledge?"

"We looked over, but there was nothing down there. If someone would have fallen over, there would have been a body on the stones below. It was getting dark, but there was still enough light for us to have seen. Terry looked around for footprints but the ground is mostly stone and hard dirt. Nothing. So we turned around, ready to leave, and I thought I heard something in the distance. Real faint, but I swear it sounded like someone laughing at us."

Cal frowned, unsure of what to make about Blake's story.

"You don't believe me, do you? You can ask Terry when he gets back. But it doesn't really matter to either of us what anyone thinks. We know what we saw. And heard."

"So what do *you* think happened?"

Blake leaned back in his chair before answering. "Growing up on the edge of town and in the hills, you get to hear stories about things. I'm sure you know what I mean, sheriff."

Cal did, and he nodded.

"People can blow them off, think what they want. But there's more folks around that have seen stuff as well. Weird things you can't explain. Well, maybe this is one of them. I don't know if it was something…natural. Maybe a guy playing tricks, but if that's so, he was damned good at it. Or maybe it wasn't natural…and it's not the kind of thing I want to deal with."

Cal said nothing.

"So it doesn't really help you out now, does it?"

"Not really," Cal replied.

"Unless you consider that what we ran into is what's responsible for all this crap going on," he added.

Blake's statement was not what he wanted to hear. There were so many unanswered questions already. The last thing he needed was a new mystery. Now it was Cal's turn to remain silent under the other man's scrutiny.

"Maybe you'll get a chance to find out the truth for yourself, if you're so inclined."

Cal stared at him, wondering where this was leading. Wherever, it was probably a place that he didn't want to go…

"Tonight, if you like." "What do you mean?"

"There's been some other trouble in the hills."
"Ramen's folk?" Cal asked, although he already knew the answer.

"Yep. They've had things going on there as well."

"Like what?"

"Like what happened some years back with that punk, Nick."

Frowning, Cal went right to it. "So what does Ramen think about all this?"

"I don't know, but if he finds out who's responsible, they'll have to answer staring down the barrel of his shotgun."

Cal had no doubt that Blake's threat was accurate.

"I told him about what happened, so he's going to the Point tonight to try and find out for himself." Cal shuddered.

The news was on TV, but Cal ignored the reporter's stoic face as he sat on his living room recliner, lost in thought. Lifting his head, he looked at the fireplace mantle, where Mindy had arranged some fall leaves and a miniature scene complete with haunted house and graves. He felt like he was in that scene right now, with so many strange things happening to him and the town. Although not one to overreact, the pressures of his job were mounting, daily. Not to mention the shadow of the Celebration hovering over him like a dark autumn cloud.

And where the hell was Sam?

Still no word from the elusive mayor. He might as well have resigned already. It was bad enough with all the crimes remaining unsolved, no true suspect materializing yet, and all the leads sketchy at best…So many things were now in motion, and Cal felt like he was trapped in the current, spinning helplessly away to wherever it would take him.

The destination was unknown.

Would he end up becoming the town mayor in reality? Or maybe public indignation would rise and swell, replacing him with some newcomer. That was highly unlikely. The pranks were malicious and annoying, but consisted mainly of damage to outside decorations, some personal property, and a few missing animals, which was pretty bad in itself. The town could survive all of this and quickly move on, once the culprits were caught.

But still…

What about the weird stories and his own experience? What could explain all of this? Blake had told a bizarre tale, one which was hard to swallow. And soon he might be discovering the truth of it for himself, as Cal had decided to meet up with the brothers tonight on an unlikely trek, with Jake in tow, hoping to find answers in the surrounding hill country, along with a possible confrontation with the unpredictable Ramen Grable.

It sounded like a chapter in some weird movie. Although Cal knew events around town never seemed to fit a well-defined script, this particular chain of circumstances had now hit a new high in the realm of the strange.

He looked at his watch, realizing it was almost time to go, the drawn curtains of the room obscuring the oppressive arms of twilight outside. It would be cool and clear this evening, he knew.

Perfect weather for chasing ghosts near Halloween...

Just then Mindy walked in, carrying a small tray with a steaming cup of coffee on it.

"Hungry for anything before you go?"

"No thanks, this will do. I gotta run soon."

Mindy sighed. "Off again. And when is Sam coming back? It's not right that you have to do his job as well."

"I have no idea. Jenn has been trying to reach him for the past few days. From what we've been told, he got caught up in some financial transactions and has been tied up. You would think a courtesy call wouldn't be out of the question." Irritated, he accepted the mug, taking a tentative sip, but as always, Mindy served the drink at the perfect temperature. He glanced at her figure, admiring the way she looked, even creeping into middle age soon.

She looked great.

"I guess I won't see you until late again."

"Probably not."

"Still no leads?"

"Not much. Seems like I turn up more questions than answers lately." Cal didn't feel like going into it any more than this, even with Mindy. How could he easily explain his own strange experiences? Well, now wasn't the time or place, and regardless, Mindy never pressed him on the details of his job -- or much else, for that matter.

Standing, he put the mug back on the tray, halffinished. Giving her a quick hug and kiss, he went over to the closet and grabbed a jacket.

"I'll see you when I come home."

Opening the front door, Mindy responded, "Be careful."

It was something she normally never had to say, and it took Cal momentarily by surprise.

"I will," he answered.

Shortly he was in his cruiser, revving the engine and pulling out of the driveway. The surrounding homes had a mixture of decorations sitting out front, although most of these were confined to porches. He knew it was from fear of vandalism, and even his own street hadn't been spared. Frank and Marcia Walker had been the latest victims, a trio of their jack-o-lanterns ending up on top of the streetlamp where he now approached. How anyone could have placed them up so high was beyond him, and without being seen yet. It could have been done very late at night, when few people were around. It served as a grim reminder as to his lack in finding the perpetrator as he passed beneath the scene. Just one more visual thorn in his side, mocking him silently that he was losing this battle. He couldn't shake the feeling that this was all connected to Nick and the Celebration, and time was running out for him to solve the crimes. He continued moving along the streets of Shington, his eyes scanning the homes and yards for anything out of place. Minutes later he reached the police station, and saw Jake leaning against a car, coming toward him when he saw Cal's approach. The big deputy opened the door and entered, and then they were off.

The Celebration

"Well, anything on Cass?"

Jake shook his head. "Nope. She wanders around a little bit at night, but doesn't seem to have any real focus. Just kind of walks about in the dark, here and there. Strange girl."

"And how reliable is Clint? He's another one you can't trust."

"If he knows what's good for him, he'll do whatever I tell him," Jake replied. Cal didn't like the sound of it, and although he hated to think it, he realized that Jake wasn't someone he necessarily trusted to do anything he was told. Over the past few years Cal had come down on the man pretty hard at times, threatening to kick him off the force if caught doing something out of bounds. So far, Cal had yet to catch him doing anything that rose to such a level. Smaller things though? Yeah.

"So this sounds like a spook chase more than anything, Cal. What do you expect to find out there tonight?"

"I really don't know. I want to see what's bothering Ramen, for one thing. I don't want him causing trouble as well. Ramen and his people have been silent for a while, and I intend to keep it that way."

"They're nothing but a bunch of ignorant hillbillies up there," Jake replied. "I wouldn't mind throwing the lot of them in jail for a while. Bust up those damn stills. That's what we need to do."

"You make it sound pretty easy. Maybe you should consider the backlash involved if we did that. People in town have close ties with his kin, and some are family. Shington isn't too bad a place to live in, and every town has its share of problems. But there are certain ways of keeping the peace, and that's something you don't know too much about, Jake."

The deputy grunted, but said nothing. Cal didn't feel like lecturing the man further, and he already knew Jake wouldn't change his opinion, which didn't matter anyway. As long as he did his job, that was good enough for Cal.

They kept driving for a while, approaching the Bentley property. Cal spotted a pair of headlights which belonged to a pickup, and slowed down. After a moment, the truck moved off, and Cal followed. It was Blake and Terry, waiting for him as they had agreed on. They drove down the road, which soon angled to the right, steeply uphill and into the encroaching forest. After about a mile, the road regressed into a mix of stone and dirt, as they now entered an area which was held by Ramen Grable and his folk. They passed a few driveways, but there were no homes to be seen, their structures lost in the distance. Posted signs were nailed everywhere, and only a fool would openly trespass in these parts. Over the years there had been several deaths in the area, and none of them had been solved. Blamed on accidental shootings, everyone knew that they were family "quarrels" of some type, and Ramen's clan dealt with such issues in their own fashion, needing no outward intervention. Cal and his police force could do little about it, and their investigations had always proved ineffective. The sheriff knew there was no way he could change the way of life here, but if anyone from town became involved, there would be major problems. He knew that Ramen was hardly intimidated by anything he could say, but Cal also knew the man would grudgingly respect the fact that Cal could go a long way in upsetting the balance in the foothills if he ever decided to bring in the state police, something he had yet to do.

The Celebration

Yeah, it was touchy ground up here.

They drove for another ten minutes and the pickup stopped, rumbling into a branch-off that looked like an oversized parking space. Both doors opened and the brothers emerged, Terry from the driver's side. Cal and Jake did the same, walking directly over to them. Jake stopped in front of Blake, folding his arms. The deputy was even bigger than the younger brother, and Cal knew that between them, they were the two men in the area whom you didn't want to mess with in a fight.

Along with himself, of course, although he was hardly someone who got into brawls, and even then, only if someone resisted arrest or took a swing at him. If this happened, he was more than capable of self-defense, and his bare hands usually served him well enough unless the situation called for his weapon. Fortunately there had only been a handful of such incidents in all his years wearing the badge.

"Terry, Blake." Cal greeted them both.

"Sheriff," Terry answered, the man a few years older than Blake, but looking a lot older. With black hair tied in a ponytail, his small black beard immediately gave him a villainous look, one which his demeanor usually reinforced.

"So you think you'll find your man tonight?" Terry grunted. He spat chewing tobacco on the ground, as if emphasizing the unspoken skepticism.

"I'm looking for answers. Whether I find the culprit tonight, who knows? If the same person is causing problems here as well, then it's my business to find that out."

Terry gave him a strange look, but said nothing else. Blake lit up a cigarette, while Jake sat down on the tailgate of the pickup. None of them seemed to have much to say, and Cal knew it was as unlikely a gathering as to be seen in those parts. They were all waiting for Ramen's arrival, and it didn't take long, as they soon heard the sound of an approaching vehicle. An old pickup drew near, parking halfway in the road, the low beams staying on, throwing off light but not in anyone's eyes. The door opened and Cal recognized Ramen Grable's scraggy face, a shotgun hanging across his shoulders. Frowning, Cal didn't want to get off on the wrong foot. He glanced over at Jake, but the deputy looked bored. He wasn't going to be intimidated by anyone. That was a certainty.

"Sheriff." Ramen approached. He was of medium build, and there was nothing about the man that spoke of his ranking among his folk. His voice was low and coarse, but there was an intensity in his eyes that made one stop before writing him off as someone to casually disregard.

Ramen wasn't someone to be underestimated, and if you did, it was at your own risk.

"Ramen. It's been a while. How are you these days?"

Cal tried to at least be courteous with the man. The last thing he wanted was to anger him, and make the whole evening a wasted effort. If there was any information these men had which could be of help, he had to find out what it was.

"Fair."

He knew that was about all he would get from the man.

"You know why we're here. There's a lot of stuff going on in town the past few weeks, and I'm having trouble pinning down whoever is causing all this. I've also heard that you might be experiencing the same kind of problems."

Ramen answered. "You heard right. And it's happened before."

There was no way of avoiding it, so Cal replied simply "Nick."

"The town couldn't keep him in line then."

Cal wondered if the man was threatening him, but he couldn't tell. "He caused a lot of trouble for everyone. It was a bad time," he replied.

"And it led to a dead body in a cold creek," said Ramen.

"Yes it did."

"Either way, he was going to find himself in a grave. You boys took care of him before I could."

"And just what are you talking about, Ramen?" This time Jake stepped in, but instead of cutting him off, Cal let him speak. "You heard me. Tire blowout at the bridge?" Ramen grunted. "Speak your mind a bit more clearly, Ramen. Nick swerved and lost control. Whether he deserved it or not don't really matter none, now does it?" Jake loomed before the man, and Cal felt the tension in the air like a living thing.

"Well, sometimes things don't end where they should. And justice has a way of setting things right." Ramen stared at Jake, clearly undaunted.

Cal knew it was time to defuse the situation before it became worse. "What do you mean by that, Ramen? I think there's a connection to Nick here for sure. Someone either has an axe to grind, or wants to pick up where he left off. Follow right in his footsteps."

"Is that what you think, sheriff? Or just what you want everyone *else* to think? That all that's going on here?"

Cal nodded. Now it was his turn to lock gazes with the unpredictable man. Cal felt uncomfortable, but wasn't about to show any sign of weakness. Too much depended on him. There was a thinly-veiled threat beneath Ramen's words, one which sounded a lot like an accusation. And it was directed either at himself or Jake. Or both...

"Maybe we'll see for ourselves tonight, if we're lucky. What do you think?" Ramen said.

"Chasing ghosts? Maybe you should lay off that rotgut whisky." Jake scowled. Cal knew his deputy was deliberately provoking the man further, and he noticed Terry's hand moving a hair closer to his pocket.

"That's enough!" Cal stepped between the two. "We came up here to see if you knew anything that could help us out in our investigation. And Jake, if you don't shut the hell up, you can go sit back in the car. That's an order, do you hear me?"

The big deputy's eyes smoldered, but it appeared he was finished. "Yes, sir," was all he said.

Ramen spoke. "Sheriff, you can look all you want. But if you want to hear what I think, listen up."

"I'm all ears."

Ramen continued. "I think something's returned to town again, stuck its nose in the air, and has come back looking for vengeance. Something bad."

"Hmmph. Back to ghosts again." Cal sighed.

"I ain't calling it anything. A man can call something any word he wants, once he's seen it himself. That's why I don't give it a name. I haven't seen nothing with my own eyes that I can't explain, but that doesn't change the feeling I have in my gut, the way my folk been acting. They're scared, and by hell, I can't allow that."

The Celebration

"I don't feel like arguing anymore." Cal held up his arms. "And I can't afford to talk away the night. There's work to do, and someone is responsible for all the trouble. Yours and mine…I know you run this neck of the woods, but you're still under my jurisdiction, and I've sworn to uphold the law. Now, are we going to look around or not?"

Ramen glanced at the brothers. Blake fidgeted, while Terry angled his head, scanning the dark forest.

"Let's get this the hell over with then," Ramen said.

Ten minutes later found the five men moving through the trees in single file, Terry and Blake leading with their own high-powered flashlights. Ramen was next, with Jake bringing up the rear. Not a word had been spoken since they left the road and their vehicles behind. The hillside was dark but not silent. Crickets chirped from grassy areas while grasshoppers buzzed from their hiding places. Overhead other insects, katydids and leaf hoppers, droned away, and Cal heard the last vestiges of the warm season in their muted calls. Every day that passed by signaled the onset of coming winter, and it wouldn't be long before the insects were finished for the year.

Cal had mixed feelings about it. The winter didn't bother him, but the fall was a time of year when his past reared up, and he found himself questioning decisions he'd made, some that he would take back if possible. But that was what the past was all about –

one's personal history, with no way to change anything. You could move forward and learn from it all, but once an act was done, it was part of your living resume, for good or bad.

Yeah, he wouldn't be sad once fall and October were behind him again.

Ramen turned around to face him. "It's just up ahead here. Terry, wait."

The brothers stopped, both drawing near. Ramen spoke again. "I don't know what we'll find out here. Probably nothing but trees and sky. But in case someone is wandering around, it might be best for us to split up. Come at the Point from both directions. That way if there is someone in the area, they won't be able to get by us."

Cal nodded. "Seems like a good idea. Jake and I will come at it from the right, you three from the left. Sound like a plan?"

Ramen agreed, and the Bentley brothers said nothing, which the sheriff assumed was meant as giving their consent. He quickly scanned their faces, reading the nervousness in their eyes and expressions. Clearly, these two were reluctant to be out here. Whatever they had seen or heard before had left a mark on them, and Cal didn't believe that they were this good at acting. And for what purpose would that be? To lead him on a wild goose chase? That made no sense at all. Rough men of this type were not apt to show weaknesses of any kind…but he had to find out what was spooking the hill folk so much.

They broke away as planned, all of them with flashlights gleaming in the gloom. Moments later Cal and Jake were moving through the woods on their own, the others disappearing as if they were forest wraiths.

The Celebration

Cal spun around, his face angry. "Damn it, Jake. When will you learn to keep your mouth closed? These people are actually cooperating for once, and you almost blew our chances of working with them."

"I don't trust any of them. They're up to no good."

"It's not your job to trust them. It's my decision, all right? We're getting nowhere with any of our leads. You haven't come through, and I haven't found anything that can nail someone. Until we do, every possible angle needs to be flushed out. You hear me?"

Jake's head drooped down, but Cal was sure it was only to hide the man's anger. What had gotten into him so much? Well, there was no sense to argue further, and time was pressing against them.

"Pay attention now and let's see what we can find out. We can talk later over a beer if you want."

"All right. No worries."

They moved off again. The pair went cautiously ahead, Cal limiting his flashlight to the ground immediately before them, not wanting to alert anyone who might be hiding in the area. He really wanted to get this over with quickly, feeling more and more that there would be no answers to be found. Blake's story had way too many holes in it to be of any help. Why, they could have seen or heard anything in these woods near nightfall.

It was the most logical explanation, except that Cal's mind refused to brush it off so easily. Deep down, he wanted it proven to be nonsense, or whisky, but the fact of the matter was that these men knew the woods and hills like no other, and there was nothing he could tell himself that would erase that reality. If they were genuinely spooked, there was a reason behind it.

Paul Melniczek

Something *strange was going on here…*

Without realizing it, Cal found himself suddenly looking at the open sky. They had reached the Point, and his head angled skyward as he saw the tiny glimmers of stars growing brighter in the autumn horizon. He glanced over to his left, spotting movement. Terry emerged from the treeline, followed by his brother and Ramen, bringing up the rear. Cal was ready to give a short yell of recognition but he stopped in his tracks as he saw the other men reacting to something which grabbed their attention, and it was then that the sheriff noticed the dim figure standing on the edge of the Point…

"What the hell…" Jake whispered behind him, but Cal ignored him. Someone was there in front of them, perched over the ledge like a predatory bird, hands extended to either side, back towards them. Chills ran along Cal's skin at the bizarre sight, and it was about the worst vision he could have imagined seeing out there on the lonely hillside. The forest grew hushed around them, and the lack of noise only added to his trepidation. The crickets and other insects had gone mute, the only sound coming from his own breathing, and Jake's beside him. And as he stared intently at the figure, he recognized the same black jacket that he'd seen on the intruder at the graveyard.

There was no question – it was the same person, and he knew without a doubt that this was the one

The Celebration

connected with all the strange happenings in the town and in Ramen's country as well.

Both groups remained silent, no one willing to break the heavy silence and shatter the trance. In the background Cal watched as the moon appeared, nearly full, adding its own magical presence to the strange scene, the shadows growing deeper. The person then lowered his arms, and a quiet laughter drifted backwards, one filled with nothing but contempt. Cal placed a hand on his weapon, uncertain of what exactly was going on here. He chanced a glimpse over to the others, but none of them had moved, even the stoic Ramen holding his stance, his shotgun untouched.

Cal had to do something – it was getting unbearable. The air was filled with tension, and the figure didn't seem to have a care in the world as to the onlookers. The men greatly outnumbered the stranger, but he felt the promise of danger here despite that fact. He felt threatened, almost as if from a psychological attack of sorts. It was one of the weirdest moments in his life, and he really had no previous background to call upon. This was something different, totally unlike the normal events that he'd become used to as sheriff. His inner senses tingled with warning, and he was frustrated as to explain any of it away…

Cal was about to say something when the figure suddenly turned, facing them. From this new perspective, it was clear that the person was some man of indeterminate age, his face concealed by shadows, and there was no mistaking the resemblance to the stranger in the graveyard…it was the same person. Without warning, the man lifted a hand in the air, holding it in front of him. They all watched as one finger jutted outwards, moving slowly towards where Cal and Jake were standing. When it stopped at their vantage point, Cal felt a spike go through his chest, as if an invisible nail had been driven through his heart. It lasted only for a moment, and then the man lowered his arm again. He then placed both hands on his hips, and did something that none of them were prepared to witness – he leaped backwards and plunged straight over the edge of the Point…

Jake gasped next to him, grabbing him on the shoulder so tightly that it hurt. Several seconds passed and Cal remembered to breathe, stunned by what he'd just seen.

He jumped over the cliff! What the hell?

"Did you see that?" Jake shook him. "Did you?"

"Yeah…" Cal replied, but his voice was no more than a hoarse whisper. Finally, he shrugged off the shackles of his inaction and moved cautiously over to the edge, flashlight illuminating the rocky outcropping where the man had stood only seconds ago. From the corner of his eye he saw Ramen and the two brothers approach, even more slowly than he had done. Cal leaned over the edge, not wanting to expose himself any more than necessary, scanning the rocks below for signs of the body. There had been no cry of anguish, not a sound, and all of them knew that it was impossible for someone to survive such a fall.

Impossible…

It had been suicide to do such a thing, and now Jake crouched alongside him, peering downwards with his own light. And they saw… …nothing.

The cliff below was void of anything save for rocks and dirt, one or two scrub bushes digging into the hard ground in their fight against gravity. Cal's throat was parched and he kept swallowing, unwilling to even blink, as he searched for a glimpse of what *had* to be

The Celebration

lying down there on the slope -- the broken body of the man.

But there was absolutely nothing to be seen.

"It's impossible. Nobody could survive that. Where's the damn body?" Jake swore next to him, and Cal looked at his face. His eyes were wide and staring, his features drawn tight in the blend of twilight and milky luminescence.

Now Ramen knelt down next to him, the Bentley brothers a few steps away from the ledge. "Save us all," Ramen said. "He's come back."

"There has to be some logical explanation for all of this." Cal stood up, inching away from the precarious ledge. "Some trick that we can't see. No one could survive a fall like that, do you hear me? No one."

"That's what I'm trying to tell you, sheriff. But you won't listen. *He's* back."

Jake spun around, his face turned to Ramen. "Who are you talking about, Ramen!" He shouted at the man, enraged. "Why don't you just say it!"

"It's him. Nick. What more proof do you need?" Jake grabbed Ramen by the shoulders, moving so fast Cal couldn't have stopped him if he'd wanted to.

"That's enough of your crap. He's dead, and there's nothing in the world that can change that. You hear me?" The two were dangerously close to the edge, and Cal was shocked by Jake's reaction. Even the Bentley brothers seemed unable to act.

"Whoa! Jake!" Cal yelled at the deputy, but didn't want to come any closer. It had suddenly become a dangerous situation and he had to defuse it. Immediately.

"Get your hands off me, you sonofabitch." Ramen struggled but was no match for the much more powerful Jake. Blake moved a step closer, but Terry seemed unable to do anything except stare at them both. "Jake, if you don't back down *now* you're done! Do you hear me?" Cal inched towards him, and Jake seemed to move nearer the edge. Did he mean to throw the man *over*?

Then just like that, Jake eased his grip, pushing Ramen towards the brothers. "You're not worth it. Any of you." He stared the trio down, defying any of them to act. Moments later he moved away from the ledge, returning to Cal's side.

"Trying to play us for fools. Wasting our damn time out here, Cal. Well, I'm not buying any of it." He turned, heading back towards the woods, but stopped in his tracks.

A sound drifted upwards from the cliff below. Cal froze, looking at the others for their reaction. They all heard it.

Laughter. Coming from below.

It lasted for a few brief, uncertain seconds, the men all standing motionless, entranced by the sound. And then, as soon as it had started, it was over. The landscape was cast in a pall of heavy silence once more, the night closing in.

But they had all heard it.

Just as Blake had told them earlier. Quiet, mocking laughter. Cal's heart pounded in his chest and he felt the unpleasant sensation of clammy sweat along his back. It was surrealistic, watching as the figure had jumped off the cliff, disappearing without a trace. There was no possible explanation for it, unless it was some kind of outrageous trick being played on them. But how was it possible? There were dozens of yards below the edge with nowhere to hide, even if someone had managed to have a rope tied fast. Where could they have gone to so quickly?

He knew it was impossible. There was no way someone could have pulled it off. But his mind swirled around in confusion, because if there was no deception involved, then that left only one other conclusion...

That something extraordinary was at play here. Something that defied all explanation. And *that* was a notion that he didn't want to entertain.

He snapped out of his reverie, knowing that he had to take action or lose his mind. "Jake! Let's go around and work our way to the bottom. There has to be something we're missing here."

He tried to keep the fear from showing in his voice, but didn't know how successful he was from doing so. The big deputy nodded, moving into the treeline. Cal glanced over at Ramen and the others, but they made no motion to join him. He knew they had all arrived at the same conclusion.

But Cal wasn't about to do the same...

Cal followed after Jake's broad form, and he heard Ramen's voice in the background. "Nick's come back, sheriff. You're not going to find anything down there except your own death."

And that was it. Cal bit his lip, feeling a wave of anxiety wash over him. He was a professional, someone who took his office seriously in upholding the law. He possessed a wealth of experience to draw from, but there was nothing he'd ever faced before that could help him now.

Retreating into the woods, the two of them scanned the trees and bushes with their lights, Cal feeling more comfort in taking action as opposed to staying at the Point and embellishing all the horrid possibilities of what they had all just seen. Events had taken a drastic turn for the worse. He had no idea as to what exactly had taken place, or what was going on around town. The only rational notion he could cling to was that someone was going to incredible lengths, using elaborate and dangerous methods to spook them, to frighten the entire town into submission, all in Nick's name.

Someone was either that damn good, or... Best not to think further on it.

They continued on for several minutes, angling their way down towards the base of the cliff. Cal had regained a measure of his senses, and he signaled to Jake for a momentary halt.

"Jake. What the hell was that all about?"

"What?"

What? Cal thought. *What? Is that all he could say?*

"You know what I mean. You damn near threw Ramen over the edge, man. What the hell's wrong with you? You lose your damned mind?"

Jake turned around, lowering his light to the forest floor. "They're in on it. Ramen and his boys. Trying to make us out for fools."

"You think they're behind all the trouble?" Cal wasn't buying it.

"Yeah."

"But why? What do they have to gain? And I don't see what any of this is meant to do...Scare us? For what reason?" He shook his head.

But Jake didn't answer his questions. "Did you hear him accusing us? Blaming us for Nick's death? He's not going to get away with it."

The Celebration

Cal listened to the deputy's words, but nothing became any clearer. Ramen had made accusations at them, and they *had* been involved in the fatal chase after Nick those years past. It was a dark passage in Cal's own life and the town's. A place that no one wanted to revisit. And yet, this past month had seen history repeating itself unpleasantly, weaving into those dark days and hanging a black cloud over the month of October. Halloween and the Celebration loomed before Cal now, coming faster with each passing day, the events becoming more bizarre and surreal, and Jake was behaving as strangely as the other weird stuff going on. What exactly was he getting at?

"Let's go. We're not going to see anything down there in this darkness anyway. Whoever it was is gone." And just like that Jake turned, heading off once more. Cal stared at the man's back for several seconds, remembering the circumstances of Nick's demise and all the events surrounding it. Memories he would rather have left to rest.

Now it seemed more likely that there had never been any rest for it at all. Only a slow, patient dormancy.

Waiting to come awake.

An hour later, Cal and Jake were sitting at the Shington Inn, drinking mugs of beer and talking about the night's events.

They had been unable to come up with anything which could shed light on what they had seen. For the hundredth time, Cal found himself shaking his head, wondering what had taken place -- the man out there on the edge of the Point, jumping backwards and going over the cliff like a diver on the high board.

Insane. Impossible.

Yet it had happened, with five witnesses there as spectators. There was no discounting the reality of it all. Not unless he was about to discredit his own eyes and ears. His mind? Well, maybe that was suspect already.

"All right. Here's the game plan." Cal spoke up, Jake watching him, his face unreadable.

"The pranks and general mischief have been going on. Fortunately, nothing worse has happened, and I guess for that we should be thankful. Neither of us know what we saw tonight. I'll go as far as that. But this guy is responsible for all that's going on around here. I don't know who it is, or how they've managed to pull all this off. But you can count on it. We saw our man out there."

Jake was silent.

"Since we've come up empty for weeks now despite a few leads, I doubt we're going to catch him before Halloween. He has more than a few tricks up his sleeve, that's for damn sure. I don't know what he did out there tonight, but I won't underestimate him. We need to focus on the Celebration and making certain that everything goes smoothly. Only a fool would think that this guy isn't trying to follow in Nick's footsteps." The deputy nodded.

"So that means he'll try something there. I want you to be on site from early in the morning until everything is shut down. Do you hear me?"

"Yeah."

"Anything strange or out of place needs to be dealt with. You call me at the first sign that something unusual turns up, or someone acts out of character. I'll check in when I can, but I'm worried about Sam. He still hasn't returned. I'm going over to his house later."

"All right. Sounds like a good idea. But what if he doesn't show up?"

"Well, then I'll be filling in as best I can, I guess." Cal shook his head, taking a swig from his mug. He continued. "And I'll be making some rounds. I've ruled out Cass, but I want to talk with her before then. I'm sure she has nothing to do with all this, but that doesn't mean she's totally innocent. That girl might know who's really behind all this."

"If that's true, she hasn't led us to him. I know Clint is keeping an eye on her."

"Even so…" Cal shrugged. "Anyway, it's going to be really busy for us the next few days. Don't plan on getting much sleep after tonight." Jake grunted.

"And another thing. That had better be the last time I ever see you go off the handle like that." This was the crux of the conversation. Cal had been leading up to it for a while, and while he trusted Jake to follow orders, he knew the man had a wild side that would never be completely tamed, and that was a problem which had some potentially serious implications.

The deputy stared down at his own mug.

"I'll tell you this now, Jake. You ever pull something like that again and I'll nail your ass to the wall. You're finished in law enforcement. I know we've worked together for years and are friends, but you crossed a line tonight. I will *not* have that on my force. Not now, not ever. You understand?"

They locked gazes, and Jake nodded. "Yeah." Cal didn't want to discuss it any further. He was a man who kept his word, and everyone knew it.

"All right. Tomorrow I'll be all over town. I'm not giving up on finding this bastard, but there's only so much I can do about it. The Celebration is going to eat up all my time right now. I wish they would just stop having the thing. Nothing but trouble."

"You don't have to tell me."

"But that's out of our hands. We need to do what we're paid for, and what the town expects from us. Basically, keeping them happy, but not *too* happy. It's getting late, and I still have things I need to do. Why don't you make a sweep on your way home, keep your eyes open for any trouble, and I'll see you in the morning."

"Good enough." Jake emptied his mug.

"Get out of here. It's been a crazy night." "Yeah, it has. See you tomorrow then, Cal." He stood up, a few heads turning their way quickly, and looking away just as fast.

Cal watched his large frame heading towards the door, still wondering about the man. Things were not adding up. He didn't question the relationship of current events to what Nick had done. That was beyond doubt. But why had Ramen accused them directly, setting Jake off in a rage? What exactly did he suspect, or know?

The sheriff leaned back in his chair, his mind going around in circles. He thought back to that night years ago, and the events played over in his head. Back to that fateful night...

Several of them had been on duty at the Celebration, including himself, Jake, Marshall, and Perkins, who had been off duty, and had since moved out of Shington, his whereabouts unknown. The evening had all started as normal – the parents showing up, the kids with the annual costume party first, a tradition before the other events took place. There had been no indication that anything was wrong. The food stands were bustling, the vendors selling their wares. The vegetable and harvest exhibits had the usual throng of people coming to and fro, as rivals suspiciously eyed each other while sitting comfortably behind their props. A band played on the flatbed, while a crowd gathered in the street, many of them with chairs put out ahead of time. The beer wagon was packed early as the power drinkers set up their positions, some of the more aggressive ones growing louder with each downed mug.

But Marshall and his officers had expected all this, and there were no surprises. It was the normal atmosphere for the big event, with its normal set of problems.

Until smoke emerged from the main tent, and people started running out, coughing and screaming.

Then, panic had ensued, and people were yelling and pushing, all of them trying to put as much distance between themselves and the source of the fire. A siren roared and the local volunteers went into action, while the officers did their best to contain the chaos.

It was then that Jake had caught a glimpse of Nick behind the largest tent, running with a bag across his shoulder. Calling to the others, they sprang into action and the chase was on. It seemed the town's most notorious troublemaker had been caught redhanded and was on the verge of making good on his escape. His Nova was parked in a nearby alley and he quickly got in, peeling off and racing away. The officers managed to put tire to the asphalt moments later and three vehicles were screaming out of town, two in pursuit of one.

Cal was in one squad car, while Marshall and Jake had the lead. They sped after Nick for a while, as he played a game of cat and mouse with the officers, but that plan turned out to be his undoing, as Jake turned off and headed for the main road out of town, guessing that Nick would eventually make a permanent run for it and leave Shington in his dust. Cal continued to follow, losing him in the twilight, but decided that the chase would end up outside of town shortly. When Cal finally caught up with Nick at the bridge it was too late, as the Nova was in the creek upside down. Cal still remembered the image as he jumped out of the car, with Jake standing there with arms crossed, shaking his head.

Nick was dead.

It was a fitting end to the troubled youth's life, and all of them knew it. They all agreed that a tire had blown and Nick's car had spun out of control, taking him over the rim and plunging to his death. Marshall had little to say, except that the episode was finished.

And that was pretty much it…the story was complete, the book closed.

Cal sat there for another minute, his mind still unraveling that last chapter.

Cal sat in the bar for another half hour, lost in thought, before he finally emerged into the late October night once more, making his way over to the cruiser. As he reached inside his pocket for the keys, a shadow loomed before him and he caught his breath in surprise.

"Still jumpy I see."

Cal went into a defensive posture, but relaxed as he recognized who it was.

Cass...

"That's a bad habit you have there, sneaking up on police officers at night. One of them is liable to pull a gun on you, you know."

The girl shrugged. "Maybe they shouldn't be out at bars while on duty."

Cal didn't like the accusation. "I'm on duty every hour of the day, and don't lecture me on drinking. I already sacrifice a good chunk of my free time for this job, and keeping the town safe. Try to find someone who has ever seen me unfit for duty because of drinking a beer or two."

"I have better things to do with my time. And that's something I want to talk with you about."

He wondered how the girl knew he was here, or maybe it was just coincidence. But then, the bar was only a few blocks from where she lived, so it was hardly a leap for either possibility.

"So talk. I'm all ears."

"You can stop having that pig Clint follow me around, for one. I'm guilty of nothing, like I told you before. He does a lousy job of it anyway." She laughed. "What a loser. He gives up pretty quick. I don't know whether he's more afraid of me now or that ape of yours Jake."

Cal considered her words. He was convinced that she wasn't behind any of the acts of vandalism, and for sure it hadn't been Cass at the Point earlier. Still...

"Hmm, you seem preoccupied, sheriff." Cal was silent.

"Seen a ghost, perhaps?"

His eyes widened, and he felt a familiar chill go down his spine.

"There's no sense in denying it anymore. I can see in in your face. In your eyes. You've *seen* him…"

Damn, he thought. *She knows something. And what could he hope to gain by lying to her now? Maybe she wasn't responsible, but she knew who had been out there.*

"I've seen him. Tonight."

Her face seemed to light up, even in the pale twilight of the nearby streetlamp. A huge grin crossed her face.

"He's come back, you know. It's Nick."

"I don't know who it was out there. But I'll get him."

Now she laughed hard. "You can't catch a ghost, sheriff! You're still denying it, after what you saw? He's back! He's come back for me!"

Cal still didn't know what he was dealing with, but he figured it would be best to play along, see what he could find out from the girl. "I suppose you've talked to him then?"

Her demeanor changed instantly, and her normal, unreadable face took over again. "No. But I've seen him in the fields, heard his voice whispering my name. It's Nick. I know it."

"And you think he's going to take you with him? If he's a ghost, then how is that possible?" Cal folded his arms.

"I don't know, and I don't care. He's here again, and that's all that matters."

"I don't think so. If what you say is true, then what's he waiting for? Why not sweep you up in his arms and you can both float away, happily ever after and all that stuff? Just like in the fairytales."

The Celebration

The bait worked, and Cass grew angry. "He's not ready yet, sheriff. There's another reason that he's back."

"And what could that be?"

"For revenge. On those who killed him."

"Killed him? Oh really?"

"Yes. And since you're standing here now, I can see that he still has some work to do."

Cal sat in his cruiser which was parked outside the front of the mayor's property, looking to see if Sam's car was there but it was empty. Still feeling shaken from the conversation with Cass, he remained sitting patiently for several minutes, debating on what to do next. The house appeared dark and vacant, and although late, if Sam *was* around, he surely would have lights on somewhere in the place. Without any word or message from the mayor, Cal had no choice but to hope that the man would still show up in time for the Celebration, which was nearly on them. He didn't believe that he would just have skipped out on them like that, never to return. He had his salary to collect and a large home here, which was worth pretty much.

No, it made no sense at all.

Frowning, Cal looked at his watch. He was tired, mentally and physically. It had been one hell of an evening, that was for sure. Meeting up with Ramen and the Bentley brothers, the incredible scene at the Point, Jake's bizarre behavior, and the chance (or not) encounter with Cass, had all stretched him to his limits.

He had half a mind to go around back and see if Sam's car was there, but at the moment, he really needed some sleep more than anything. If he was able to, that was.

Well, there was always tomorrow morning with the hope of a new day, and possibly some informative revelations. Man, he could certainly use them right now.

Yawning, he turned around and entered the main street, the car misfiring as he went around a corner. It needs a tune up, he thought. Just like *I* do. Keeping his eyes open for signs of any unusual activity, he moved slowly through the streets of Shington, steadily making his way back to his own home, and one he found himself missing more and more as of late. And Mindy. He could always rely on her being there for him, no matter his mood. She knew when he was under a lot of stress, or had a bad day at work, and she possessed an uncanny skill at knowing exactly what to say, or what *not* to say. He respected and loved her for that quality, and many others as well. A soft smile spread across his face, thinking how nice it would be to just collapse and fall asleep in her arms. A twinge of guilt played at him also, thinking how lucky he really had it, and that he had not always appreciated her and his life as he should have. He tried to live his life by doing what was right, but no one was perfect.

People made mistakes.

He had made mistakes in the past.

And his greatest fear, at that moment, was that the shadows of his own past had materialized again to haunt him, in the form of an elusive and mysterious being who was doing his best to reincarnate Nick in the flesh.

Cal had been connected to Nick and the circumstances of his death, and as much as he wished it to be otherwise, there was simply no way of erasing the past.

When he pulled into his own driveway, his mind swirled with so many thoughts and emotions that he felt a headache coming on. It really was time for some rest, and the last thing he wanted to do was lay awake and wrestle with his conscience. He'd done it many times before – sometimes calling a truce, admitting his errors and promising never to commit them again, but other times he'd been beaten badly, deserving the harsh reality of self-rebuke.

Ah hell, he thought…

He opened the front door, moving inside beneath the glare of lamps that were always on after dusk. He felt a slight twinge of hunger and went directly to the kitchen, finding a sandwich for just an occasion, made of course by Mindy. Sitting for a minute, he consumed it quickly, dashing it down with a glass of orange juice. Satisfied, he half-undressed and made his way quietly upstairs where his wife was surely in bed by now. The door to the bedroom was open, the lights out. As he entered, he heard the sound of her light breathing, feeling comfort in the familiar noise. Easing himself down, he lay next to her, able to put his body at ease after all the day's events. His mind was another matter, and it was a while before that finally shut down, allowing him to fall asleep, but his dreams were restless that night, filled with vague images and beings which tormented him relentlessly.

The following morning found Cal awake early and bustling around the house, Mindy already gone for work. *So much to do,* he thought, *and such little time to do it in.*

The Celebration and All Hallow's Eve were tomorrow. He was amazed by that fact. Tomorrow. And it wasn't like the orange and black holiday had come sweeping by unexpected, catching everyone by surprise like some years. No, this past October had dragged along, filled with bizarre events and malicious acts, catching him in its inevitable wake. If Halloween truly had two sides, one of a light and the other dark, then its uglier face had descended on Shington, intent on unleashing its malevolent spooks and goblins upon the earth once more to cause as much chaos and damage as possible.

The pranks had gone on the entire month, and his inability to solve them and prosecute the culprit had failed. Yet he had witnessed something incredible last night, and the image of the man jumping backwards over the cliff was vivid in his mind's eye. It had been either the most elaborate and dangerous stunt he'd ever seen, or…

And there it was again. That *other* explanation, the one that Ramen Grable and the Bentley brothers had embraced without hesitation – that Nick had returned from the grave, seeking vengeance on the people who had been involved in his death. Cal was certainly not prepared to go down that entire path, although it would be pure ignorance to deny that someone was following in Nick's footsteps.

And Jake? He didn't believe in the supernatural explanation.

Still…

The Celebration

Cal slumped into the kitchen chair, draining the rest of his coffee, wondering how all this would end. He knew it would be soon; he could feel it in his blood. Something sinister was in the air, and was about to take further action. The Celebration was the obvious target, and Cal was prepared to meet it head on. Jake would be on patrol over there today and tomorrow, until the damn thing was over. The sooner the better. For himself, he would continue searching for the identity of the mysterious man behind all the trouble. The guy was clever and obviously had hidden talents, but Cal also thought he was overconfident. That stunt at the Point had been impressive, and spoke of someone who was afraid of nothing.

Hell, he had no idea how it could have been pulled off, but he hoped that it would lead to his slipping up somewhere and an eventual downfall, and that's when *Cal* would be waiting for him.

Standing, he grabbed a bag from the table filled with several items for the day's work, food included. Locking up, he soon was outside in the brisk autumn air. Chilly and cloudy, it certainly felt like Halloween. The neighborhood decorations added to it, but even without their misshapen forms and faces, Halloween made its presence known. Its breath was in the biting air, its arms hidden among the dried and scattered leaves. Its shadow was behind every tree and fence, and its firefly eyes were in the gleaming, sputtering candlewicks of jack-olanterns as they were lighted every night. You could smell it from wood burning stoves and chimneys, or far away piles of leaves smoldering into ash.

Halloween was all around him, and wasn't about to let Cal forget it.

The drive to the station went by quickly as he was consumed in deep thought. When he entered the station, Arlene was already at her desk, simultaneously handing him several notes scratched on pads and a steaming cup of coffee. He was always on time, and his secretary was always ready for him.

"Good morning, sheriff. Looks like another busy day for you."

"Nothing new there," he mumbled. "Any word from Sam?"

"Not a peep."

He shook his head. "Honestly, I think he wants to kill two birds with one stone. Or one announcement...Get the Celebration over with and his retirement started. But I can't believe he would leave us hanging like this for days."

"It's not like him, that's for sure."

"No it's not...hold all my calls. I'll only be in my office for a little while."

"All right," Arlene replied. "And Jake's been in and out already. He's going straight over to the square."

"At least someone's on the ball..."

Shutting the door behind him, Cal placed the mug on his desk and sat down. Scribbling on his own notepad, he wanted to make sure he didn't forget anything. His schedule was hectic enough.

And Sam? What was he thinking?

He jotted down the following: *Head over to Sam's.*

Even though he had pulled up to the mayor's house last night, he was going to check around back as well this time. Retiring or not, it was still out of character for Sam not to return his calls after being a few days late. Cal enjoyed his job and the variety of challenges it presented him with, as long as people weren't getting hurt, of course. And he certainly looked forward to the quieter times when he could just cruise around town and make his presence known. In the end, that was always the fact which prevented most crime from ever taking place – the deterrent of law and those who were entrusted in upholding it. Unfortunately, the combined aspects of both administrative and functional duties were overwhelming him with the mayor still unreachable.

He shook his head in frustration, worried about Sam. No one in town would be happier than he, once October, Halloween, and the Celebration were all over.

And especially once the perpetrator of all the pranks was brought to justice, of course.

Rubbing his eyes, he sighed deeply, preparing himself mentally for the day's work. Tomorrow was it -- the big day. And what would it bring? More surprises, perhaps another appearance by his nemesis, the Nick impersonator? Or would it end quietly, the vandalism over, the town falling back into its sleepy routine? Cal fervently hoped it would turn out to be the latter, but his instincts told him otherwise.

All right, all right…he could sit there all day and drive himself crazy, but that would solve nothing. Gathering his things together, he was out the door in a minute, waving one hand to Arlene. Once outside, he walked towards his vehicle, unlocking the cruiser and tossing the paperwork on the passenger seat. Cal could have leafed through it in the comfort of his office, but he felt a sense of urgency, and the longer he stayed cooped up, the antsier he became. He needed to be out on the streets, part of the action, the game. For that was what it had become now -- an ugly, frustrating game, with him on one side of the tugging rope and the unknown culprit on the other.

And one of them would lose.

Cal shuffled through the notes, which consisted of several new complaints about vandalism, and he placed these to one side. He then noticed a letter hailing from Arizona, the sender one Sheriff Gonzalez, whom he'd spoken to a few weeks before. Curious, Cal opened it, silently reading the note contained within, his mouth opening in surprise at what it revealed. He looked up, staring at the quiet neighborhood around the station, his eyes glazed over.

It seemed that Nick's brother, Carson, had recently escaped from prison and was now on the loose.

Carson was out of prison!

The one person who could possibly cause all the trouble plus have the motivation for doing so was free. Nick's older brother, Carson. He'd been one of the first people that Cal had suspected, and now Carson was out of jail, his whereabouts unknown.

Had he finally returned, seeking vengeance on those he believed to have caused his brother's death?

Cal thought it was a reasonable conclusion. There was no solid proof yet that Carson had returned to Shington. No one had claimed to have seen or talked to him, and the mysterious stranger with a penchant for bizarre tricks hadn't been identified. But it *might* have been Carson. Cal tried to remember everything he knew about him. He looked a lot like Nick, in both size and proportion. If they both had faced away from you and wore similar clothing, it was hard to determine one from the other.

Cal rubbed at his chin. Yes, Carson might be the one they were after. And if this was true, and Carson had returned, then most likely Cass was in on it, playing along with Nick's brother and trying to spook him and the townsfolk. A way to get back at them all, for the girl had made this all known, not bothering to hide her animosity from either Cal or anyone else. Yeah, it made a lot of sense. But to this extent? Whoever was behind all the trouble was clever, resourceful, and had a large axe to grind. Nodding to himself, Cal was convinced that the pair together was all of the above, and probably more. And they also were something else – arrogant.

Still…

At least he now had a solid lead as to a real suspect. Even so, there was little to go on. No sign of Carson, no witnesses to the actual acts of vandalism. It was true that Jake, himself, the Bentley brothers, and Ramen Grable, had all been at the bizarre scene at the Point. It was well-orchestrated, certainly. But none of them could prove who had been there, and how they'd managed to pull it off. Just the fact that Carson was out and his location unknown was enough for Cal to feel that he was close to catching the culprit, and things were drawing to a conclusion. It didn't mean he felt any more confident that the Celebration would go off without a hinge, though.

He picked up the receiver and radioed Jake. "Yeah?" The deputy's husky voice crackled from the other end.

"I have some very interesting news."

"Oh? Spill it, Cal. I'm all ears."

"Listen to this. It seems that Carson's out of jail, and they don't know where he's at."

"Carson? Nick's brother?"

"Right."

There was a pause, then a low whistle. "Then we might have our man finally."

"We just might," Cal answered.

"No other information?"

"Unfortunately, that's all I've got. We know what he looks like, of course, but that hasn't helped us so far. No one has actually seen him, or witnessed any of the crimes. And there's also the fact that no one has identified him actually being here in town."

"Well, I think we *have* seen him all right. At the Point, pulling off his little escapade."

"Yeah. He's the prime suspect at least, and if it's him, he's done a real good job at eluding us so far. I think that Cass knows all about it, though. I want you to head over there and call her bluff."

"Should I bring her in for questioning?"

"Yeah. She actually paid me a little visit last night after you left."

"Oh really?"

"She told me that Nick's back and is looking for revenge. That kind of thing...And she even threatened me, saying that he's not done yet. It was enough that I could have taken her in last night, but thought better to keep her on the loose for the moment."

"I would say so...the girl's got a mouth on her, and some nerve."

Thinking about it now, Cal realized that the girl *did* have a lot of nerve. Making an indirect threat against the town sheriff was pretty serious stuff. The girl was way overconfident, and possibly dangerous as well.

Yeah, the cards seemed to be finally falling into place. It was time for him to make his move.

"I want you to go over there right now. No rough stuff either, and don't make a scene."

"Of course not."

"Call me when you get back to the station. I have a lot on my plate today."

"Will do. And what about here? We still need to keep a watch on this place."

"Well, hopefully he'll get careless and someone will see him. Those brothers aren't easily forgotten. And that kind of arrogance will be their undoing, I think."

"Sounds good. I'll see you then."

"All right." Click.

Cal's mind was racing and he felt a surge of excitement, now that he had a firmer grasp on the situation. Maybe things would pan out after all, and the Celebration would go off without a hitch, leaving Carson to fall short of Nick's ability to create such chaos.

Maybe...

But there were still unanswered questions, and the main suspect was somewhere loose in the area, most likely very close by. On a whim, he decided to drive by the flower shop, and check in on Mindy. Several minutes later he parked the cruiser outside the shop, and he peered inside, where he caught a glimpse of his wife as she waited on a customer. He felt a twinge of guilt, knowing that he was damn lucky to have someone who loved him that much. He wanted to go inside and talk to her, but noticed several other people walking around with items in hand, waiting to purchase them or perhaps ask questions. She looked pretty busy. The police side of him was concerned, with today being what it was, and a troublemaker still at large, but he didn't think she was in any danger. And he could help to make the situation much better by spending his time trying to catch the culprit. Sighing, he pulled away, but with some reservation. Almost as an afterthought he wondered about Sam, and if the missing mayor was returning to host the festivities.

Or if he was all right.

That notion bothered him, and he decided to head directly over to the man's house, and give it a good once over. Driving through the streets, he saw that most homes and businesses were decked out for the holiday. Plastic pumpkins dangled from lamp posts, porches were littered with jack-o-lanterns and cornstalks, and a variety of yard decorations were out in full force despite the recent vandalism. The malicious acts hadn't accelerated or tapered off, but had been uniformly committed, scattered all over town. It seemed no neighborhood had been immune from the destruction, while none had been excessively singled out. But there had been dozens of incidents the entire month, with no one coming forward and claiming to have seen the perpetrator. The only sightings had all been pretty strange -- from Ray at the cemetery, to the Bentley brothers and even Ramen Grable.

But one thing was certain. After this month was over, it would be a long time before he forgot this particularly dark and bizarre Halloween season.

The Celebration

Minutes later he found himself near the mayor's house, and he maneuvered the cruiser around back, where he would approach more inconspicuously. He felt the dirt from the road crunch beneath the tire's wheel, and he winded along, passing through a protective line of trees until he was within sight of Sam's house. To his disappointment, there was no vehicle to be seen. Frowning, he shut the engine off and stepped out, stretching his arms and staring at his surroundings. The mayor sure had a beautiful spot here, he thought. Cal had been there before of course, on and off business, but he never ceased to admire the convenient location and well-kept grounds.

He walked toward the home, enjoying the cool breeze playing across his face and hair. October was in the air, with all the mischief it brought. Cal had felt this same ominous feeling before, and he was uneasy with this time of year to begin with. The past had kept its skeletons in good repair, and Halloween was the prime season to bring them back into the present.

He stepped onto the porch, looking around for signs of recent passage. Trying the handle, he found that it was locked, so he banged loudly, knowing already that it was an empty gesture.

"Sam, where the hell are you?"

Cal folded his arms across his chest, realizing that the man might very well be gone for good. He walked along the porch for a moment, and then he looked down, spotting footprints leading to the door. It had rained the other day, and the marks looked fresh. It seemed that the elusive mayor might have returned to town after all, although he couldn't be sure. Anyone could have been here, but Cal doubted that they would have used the back door. Everyone knew where Sam lived, and also where his office sat.

Still...

It left him nowhere, only with more unanswered questions. His schedule was too full to add another investigation to it, unless he thought something was wrong, and there was no real evidence behind it. It was common knowledge that the mayor was looking into retiring to Florida, and had dropped plenty of hints that it might be sooner rather than later. Shaking his head, Cal had no choice left but to leave, knowing that his workload wouldn't be easing up any time soon. Returning to the cruiser, he started the engine and was soon driving through the streets of Shington once more. He slammed on the breaks as a dark figure darted out in front of him, barely missing his left front tire. *A black cat...*

"Damn," he said. "Almost got you."

The animal scurried off across someone's yard, never looking back. Cal thought about black cats and their role in superstition. It was said to be a harbinger of bad luck if one crossed in front of you. With Halloween's orange and black silhouette looming before him at every turn, he felt a sense of trepidation, something that he could have certainly done without. Not one to be overly superstitious himself, he wasn't exactly a full-blown skeptic either. Regardless, logic and reasoning usually prevailed with his decision making, and he was committed to keeping on that path. The alternative wasn't something he really wanted to consider.

Cal started the car moving again, trying to stay focused on the neighborhood around him as opposed to the endless stream of thoughts pouring through his head.

The Celebration

He kept to the edge of town, making his way steadily west, until he reached Berry Street, which signaled the end of the residential area, giving way to a mixture of fields and copses, with a scattering of homes, all of them on large plots. He drove on another mile until a lane appeared with a sign hanging limply on a wooden pole. The lettering was weathered, getting hard to make out anymore, but Cal knew the name well.

Pete's Garage.

It was as simple as that. Pete had passed away a few years back, a crusty old guy who could fix anything with an engine, and had worked on the police force vehicles along with half the other cars and trucks in town.

Cal turned right, his cruiser rumbling down the stone driveway which cut between trees and brush on either side. A hundred yards later and the garage itself appeared, a modestly-sized building which had seen its better days. Old barrels stood huddled together, rusting away and forgotten. Two stacks of wooden skids sat next to the encroaching forest, partly hidden by high grass. Random car parts lay on the ground as if thrown there to never be used again. The place had a forlorn and sad look, and Cal remembered when the property had been humming with activity, Pete and his mechanics twisting and hammering away in the main part of the garage, all of them putting as much effort into their trade as they did to their drinking. Cold beer or whisky was always on hand, where Pete kept the brews in an old upright inside. The officers had never gone thirsty while waiting for their vehicles, Cal included. After Pete had passed away, the property had gone to his son Leo, who had subsequently lost interest in being a mechanic or even working, for that matter. Last anyone knew he'd left Shington and headed east towards the coast, taking his inheritance with him and leaving behind the garage and property. Cal knew that taxes were overdue and it was simply a matter of time until the local township would seize it, and then it would be their problem. People weren't flocking into Shington and business had a tendency to remain flat, with most folk content on things staying as they were. That's what Shington was at its core -- a small, out of the way town that had little interest in the outside world. And every year a few more people drifted away, breaking free of the soft, invisible shackles which could lure you into complacency, and perhaps even contentment for some.

Yeah, Cal remembered old Pete quite well. And now the man was dead, his grave vandalized.

Why?

Ray had shown him the damage at the cemetery, but after his weird encounter that evening and the series of bizarre events afterwards, Cal had given the matter little thought.

So that's why he was there now.

There had been two graves violated which the old caretaker had brought to Cal's attention. Marshall's had been one, and it was easy to understand someone holding a grudge against the former sheriff. Officers of the law acquired enemies over the years. It was nothing unusual, and to be expected. And if Carson *was* the one behind all the acts of maliciousness, then it made perfect sense. He was seeking vengeance for the death of his brother, and Marshall had been the one holding office during that fateful October night. With the sheriff himself dead, his grave was chosen as a worthwhile target.

But why Pete?

The Celebration

Cal moved closer to the garage, noticing that the door was cracked open. Cautiously, he went forward, turning the knob and walking inside. He tried the switch but it was dead. Most likely the power had been turned off a while ago. The place certainly seemed deserted, and he had no reason to believe anyone else was there, lurking somewhere inside.

No reason, or maybe as much a reason as any other probability these days...

With one hand on his holster, he carefully picked his way through the building, first going through the office then into the garage itself, shining his light into every nook and corner, although there were few places to hide. Several containers and skids, engine parts and little else. The refrigerator was still there, another discard from more active times. It made him feel sad, and he suddenly realized that the town's life was unfolding before his eyes, every day, and he played as much a role in its passing as anyone. Shington wasn't necessarily dying, but it remained in a listless state more akin to a slow dance gliding towards purgatory, lulling its residents into complacency, himself included. No wonder others had left, never to return. And what about him? He considered himself a happy man, married to a wonderful wife, with a solid career and nice home.

Wasn't that enough?

He believed so, although there were moments of regret, especially this time of year. All towns had their own dark secrets, and kept them close.

He was far from perfect himself, and felt guilty as charged. That's why this time of year made him so moody, and filled with nostalgia for good, clean memories from year's gone by, before he had done the stupidest thing possible.

Cal wanted to get out of there. The garage looked empty, and the only thing he had succeeded in doing was to increase his feelings of depression. He turned around, heading back toward the door. Going through the office and outside in the cool air once more, he felt better, his spirits lifting. Wrestling with his conscience, he told himself he wasn't a bad person, but had admittedly used poor judgment in the past, vowing to improve and never make the same mistakes.

Wasn't that what being human was all about? If you realized your faults and weaknesses, you strove to overcome them and grow as a person. That was the truth he held onto, and he thought he'd done exactly that. If you didn't feel guilt, then there was no chance of redemption. A conscience kept you in check, and once fully awakened, made you think before acting. Well, it was his life, and his choices. He liked to think they had been for the better these days, not the worse.

The morning was growing late, and there were a lot of things on his plate. He thought about Pete again, and the role he'd played in Nick's death. Staring at the lot, he remembered seeing the wrecked carcass of Nick's car, the hot rod Nova, the metal twisted and broken. The vehicle had sat here for only a short while, quickly taken to the dump and disposed of. *Very quickly.*

And Pete's grave had been vandalized.

Whoever had done it must hold a special grudge against the man, and if it had indeed been Carson, then he would have connected Pete with Nick's death in some capacity.

Cal wondered how much Carson really knew.

The Celebration

The day slipped by, and Cal found himself tied up in a minor crisis. Joel Seppard's barn had caught on fire, out on the southern edge of the township. Although the building had burnt to the ground, none of the farmhands or livestock had been damaged, only property. The fire department would be in charge of investigating the cause, and eventually he left the scene for them to take over. Cal wasn't overly suspicious, since the wiring had been old, and Joel used a kerosene heater for the barn. More disturbing to him had been the inability of Jake to track Cass down. It seemed the girl was now missing, not showing up for work, and her mother had no idea where Cass was, insisting she wasn't her keeper to the deputy.

Cal now sat in his cruiser on the edge of the Shington Creek, at a small park that was popular for walkers and fishermen. At the moment the place was empty, the tranquil picture of a late October day, with colorful leaves of burnt orange and yellow clinging tenaciously to the thinning branches, prolonging their inevitable fall to the mossy ground to join their kindred. The bubbling brook was clear and inviting, and Cal took up the offer, bringing out his lunch and relaxing on one of the benches. He longed for a few minutes of quiet solitude, and was no stranger to the peaceful park. It helped soothe the stresses of his life, and right now he needed it.

Looking over at the serene water, he noticed something flashing in the sunlight, a reflection of metal in the water. He strode over to the edge, hoping to find out what it was. The place was clean, and he had no tolerance for people littering. Spotting an object in the shallows, he moved towards the spot, seeing something in the water. Reaching almost to his limit, he grabbed the guilty shard and pulled it from the cold stream. Looking at what he held in his hand, he felt his stomach churn, realizing just what exactly he'd found. It was the broken lettering for a car.

A Nova...

Cal stared down at the piece for long moments, his mind in a daze. *Was this a cruel twist of fate, or did his chance find have more behind it than pure coincidence?*

He put the piece down on the bench, lowering himself again. He closed his eyes, wondering how in the world all these strange things kept happening to him. It was too much, too weird. Shington was a quiet town, and although it had its share of abnormalities, nothing compared to this past month. Not even close.

Knowing that it was useless to beat himself up trying to understand it all, he quickly finished his meal, feeling more edgy than when he'd first arrived. It seemed there would be no rest for the weary just yet. Not until the Celebration and Halloween were over, and the true perpetrator found and brought in. Time was moving fast, and he had things to do in preparation for what the next day might bring. He had the distinct feeling that events would find a conclusion tomorrow, for better or worse.

For now, it was time to go. He would enjoy the park another time.

Cal glanced at his watch and saw that the afternoon was getting long. Then he remembered the parade.

The Celebration

"Oh, man, I almost missed it..."

He hurried to the cruiser, still holding the scrap of metal. The annual Halloween parade would be starting soon at the Shington Elementary school, and as sheriff, it was a tradition that he show up. Busy or not, he wasn't about to disappoint the kids. He only hoped they were not starting earlier than usual. Again he found himself driving through the streets of the town, and it was no surprise how much time he actually spent driving. Such was the life of a law enforcement officer, he knew...He drove a bit faster than usual and pulled into the parking lot of the school just in time, it seemed. The kids were lined up, many with parents hovering nearby, the teachers doing their best to keep the anxious children in order. Out of formality (and also to add to the excitement), Cal turned the siren on for a brief moment, then went to just flashers for effect. Some of the children clapped and giggled, their costumes flapping in the wind, while others looked on through masks, their expressions unknown. It pretty much depended on their age, as the youngest still had a sense of awe when it came to the police, and the older the child, the differing of attitudes, some obviously getting worse with age.

The parade was now officially underway, and a horde of ghosts and goblins descended on the streets of the town, making for the single family homes which sat near the school grounds. Cal angled his car into the lead, looking around for familiar faces, which he recognized. One in particular was absent, though.

Sam.

This was the last real chance where the man could still make an appearance in time and resume the callings of his office.

Better late than never.

But Cal had a sinking feeling that the mayor would do no such thing, leaving him in charge of all his affairs instead. It still made no sense, and Cal wondered again what had happened to the man.

Cal cruised slowly along, occasionally waving to people on the street. The weather was fair for this late in October – cloudy, cool, and windy, so the parade would have no issue of cancellation, and that was good. Things like this were a fun part of his job, although with his distraction from other pressing matters, he'd nearly forgotten the event. He stared in his rearview mirror, wondering what it would be like to have a child of his own back there, stomping through the streets in innocent fun.

What would Mindy think?

But he already knew the answer. She would be overjoyed. They were a happy but childless couple, and admittedly, his career had been the main reason, for the most part. Having a child was something they had never really talked too much about, deciding early on that they were fine as husband and wife. But Cal knew better. The biological clock was always ticking, and he believed that Mindy was playing the traditional wife, waiting on him.

Maybe it was time to give her what she really wanted. As he looked at the children now, he wondered what it would truly be like if his own child was there as well. A wave of emotions went through his mind, making him smile. Having their own kid might change his entire perception of October and Halloween. Even as the smile grew broader across his face, he spotted a vehicle in the background, easing into a parking space near the middle of the parade. *It was a Nova.*

A blue one...

The Celebration

Cal felt fingers of ice crawl along his spine, his body going tense. There were maybe one or two vintage Nova's in the area, and none of them were this color. It looked *exactly* like Nick's car, even from this distance. It sat in the shadows beneath a monolithic oak tree, getting smaller as he moved along leading the parade.

Was this his culprit now, making another daring move of arrogance to throw in his face? He could stop, try to direct the teachers to move the children out of the way, but it would certainly cause a lot of chaos and anxiety among the kids and parents alike. He didn't want to create a minor panic, or ruin the parade, and there was a chance that it was a harmless spectator, watching the event.

A chance, although Cal's instincts told him otherwise.

He bit his lip, trying to think it through. If he believed the children were in any danger he would have reacted instantly, but there had been no evidence that the suspect was going to do anything of that degree. From all his actions, the person was in no rush to get caught, and had covered his tracks pretty darn well.

Still weighing his options, Cal watched as the Nova backed away, doing a U-turn and disappearing from sight, as if to let their presence be known, and nothing more. If that was the purpose, it had been done well, putting the sheriff on the defensive with little option other than continuing to lead the parade. Cal knew that was exactly the reason, and the brief period of confidence he'd felt earlier had now completely vanished, leaving him with a feeling of growing trepidation.

"Happy Halloween to you too," he said. "Your arrogance will land you in my jail soon enough."

He tried to sound confident to himself, but the fact was that the instigator had been playing with an upper hand for the past few weeks, and leads or not, still remained free. Cal figured there was little he could do but continue with the responsibilities of his job, and right now that meant leading the parade around the surrounding neighborhoods and back to school safely. Several more people waved to him from the sidewalks and he waved back, although he couldn't force a smile onto his face. The minutes passed and he rolled by homes and side streets without further incident. The trappings of the season and its orange and black holiday were everywhere around him. Despite the pranks and acts of mischief, people celebrated Halloween and were not about to be intimidated. The Celebration was almost here, and the townsfolk of Shington were ready for it. It was a small community, and when the occasion gave rise for them to break from their routine, it was fully embraced. He felt like calling Jake to see if anything new had turned up, but Cal realized he was only kidding himself. The deputy would radio him first thing, so why bother. Cal needed to let events run their course. He'd done what he thought was best to track down the suspect, and getting frustrated wouldn't help his state of mind. He also believed there was a deeper connection between Nick's death and recent events, but couldn't put his finger on it yet. With all the crazy things happening lately, it was a miracle that he hadn't turned into a lunatic.

Breathing deeply, he sighed, focusing on the present. Before he knew it, the route had been completed and they were back at the school once more. He left his vehicle, waving and nodding to children, parents, and teachers alike, but thankfully no one approached him to talk. It seemed everyone had their hands full, and that was a good thing. Several minutes later he was finished there, the formality of his presence completed until next year's parade.

He wished he could take more joy from the event, but it was useless thinking about it. Time to get back to the work at hand. It was mid-afternoon, and he felt as if he'd done nothing so far. The fire earlier had tied him up, but if he were to be honest with himself, what else could he have done? Bringing Cass in would probably solve nothing until they found the true culprit. Cal doubted he could scare the girl into ratting out Carson, if he was truly responsible for the trouble. Cass had a major axe to grind, and wouldn't give in without a big fight. Despite threatening him, Cal knew that in the end it would turn up nothing. Instead of calling her bluff, she would call *his* bluff. But with her disappearance now, it only bolstered the fact that she was involved somehow. And the girl had nowhere to go unless Carson took her out of Shington for good. That would be the best thing for all of them, he realized. The girl would never be happy here, and the townsfolk were never going to accept her as one of their own. Yeah, not a bad move in all. He would certainly not pursue her if she left the area, or Carson either. Let them think they accomplished something, enacted a form of revenge, then leave and never come back. The mischief would be over, and the sleepy little town would fall back into its normal mode once more, keeping the past where it belonged.

The notion had its appeal, although it bothered Cal that criminals would go unpunished. Still, the whole idea just didn't *feel* right to him at all. He was missing something crucial, and had yet to discover just what it was.

He made his way through town, eventually reaching the square. Cars and people were everywhere. Food and game stands were mostly setup, and the beer wagon had been rolled into placed. He frowned, knowing it was more trouble than it was worth. The main tent dominated the scene, and fall decorations added flavor and color to the spectacle. He knew that people would be flocking here tonight mainly to sample the food, but the exhibits and judging all took place tomorrow. Searching around, he quickly found Jake, the big deputy talking to one of the vendors.

"Hey Cal."

Cal motioned him to the side, and Jake followed, where they could have some privacy.

"Nothing on Cass. Her mom knows nothing, and Clint claims he hasn't seen her since early yesterday."

"If we can believe him, that is," Cal muttered.

"I think so. He's been cooperating enough."

Cal wasn't so sure, but let it go. "Anything interesting happen here?"

"Nope. Everything going smoothly. Josh is stopping by her place when he can, and Marlin will drop by overnight like you told him. I still wish we had another hand to help out. It's been a lot of hours lately."

"Just think of all that overtime money. You'll be able to retire young."

"Speaking of retiring, nothing from Sam, I take it?"

"No." Cal had a lot on his mind, and the missing mayor had been out of his thoughts for a while. If we don't get anything soon, I might put out an alert for him. I hope nothing's happened."

The Celebration

"Knowing Sam, he's just fine. Getting out of town sooner than expected, or maybe that was his plan all along."

Cal knew he had a point. Sam had complained a lot the past few years, and although the job had its demands, it wasn't as if Shington were the cultural or business hub of the state. It was normally uneventful.

"I've thought the same thing. Well, we'll just have to wait and see." "So now what?"

Cal gave him a curious look. "If Carson is loose, and Cass with him, any hints on where they might be?" Jake asked.

"Obviously she won't be returning home. We'll have to talk with her mom and see if she packed her things. There's a chance she left for good, and won't ever come back."

"Hmm. That would be helpful," Jake replied. "Hey, if you're hungry, we can hit the burger stand before you leave."

"I'm sure you've been there already today."

"Nothing wrong with taking advantage of job perks, you know. I don't know why you don't do it more."

Cal shook his head. "I think I'll skip. Still have some running around to do, and the day is racing by. I want you here until close, and I'll stop by later. Keep the drunks in line, but you already know that."

"The wagon opens at five, and it *will* be closed by nine."

Cal believed him. On certain things, he trusted Jake completely.

With that, he was off again, stepping into the cruiser and making the rounds through Shington once more. He checked back into the station and Arlene drilled him with a host of messages, all of them minor, which was good. But the amount of them was bad, and he found himself spending the rest of the afternoon following up on everything from a dog that barked too much to hints of an underage drinking party before tomorrow's festivities. Cal made a dozen separate stops, and wasn't finished until after seven. When he finally returned to the police station once more he was alone, Arlene gone for the day, but leaving him with a whole new set of messages on his desk. He slumped into his chair, bone tired. This kind of stuff tended to wear you down after a while. But he was doing the job for two, while Sam had never been sheriff and mayor at the same time.

Shuffling through the messages, there didn't seem to be anything pressing, so he put them aside. Tomorrow was the big day. The Celebration was here at last, and it couldn't have arrived (and be over with) any quicker. Arlene had left the coffee pot hot, and he poured himself a large one, relaxing at his desk for a minute. He nearly spilled it when he heard a loud rumbling coming from outside, unmistakably a signature hum of a car with an aggressive engine. He went to the window and peered outside through the shades, his heart skipping a beat when he saw a classic blue Nova sitting halfway down the street.

It was the same car he'd seen at the parade. And it looked exactly like Nick's...

The car idled there, the engine revving several times. Was he being baited this openly now? Daring to park in front of the police station?

Cal was a bit spooked, finally seeing the car in the open for the first time, and recognizing it for what it was – an exact replica of Nick's car. It was as if time had backtracked on itself, and those seven years following Nick's death had never happened. It was surreal, and Cal stared out the window, unable to make out the driver from the distance and twilight.

Spooked or not, he was also angry at the arrogance of whoever was inside it, throwing their brashness directly into his face. Even though he knew what would happen, he grabbed his things and hurried to the back door, quickly locking up. As soon as he was outside and running to his cruiser, he heard the Nova peeling away, burning rubber in its wake. By the time he got down the street, the much faster car would be long gone, dodging through the lanes of Shington and disappearing. He was not going to fall for a wild goose chase, especially with it nearly dark outside. His time would come, and the ante would soon be up on the brazen perpetrator. Cal had been patient until now, and rushing headlong wouldn't resolve anything. The guy was good, along with being incredibly overconfident.

Cal bit his lip in frustration, but was determined as ever to bring the punk in. He would slip up, and then it would be over.

But not just yet...

Let Carson – if that's who it was – think he had the sheriff over the barrel, or worse yet, scared of a vengeful ghost. That would play into Cal's ultimate advantage. Someone would track him down, or rat him out. Soon.

In the meantime, Cal needed to focus on all the current activities, and be fully alert to whatever the culprit might try next, with all paths leading to the Celebration.

Cal got in the cruiser and headed directly to the town square, eager to see how things were going. When he arrived, everything appeared as expected. People walked around, shuffling between food stands and other novelties, while a throng of men (and a few women), huddled around the beer wagon, sipping from glass mugs. Cal parked directly in front of it, drawing the usual stares, which he ignored. Jake's car was parked behind the tents on the other side, where he could get away quickly if he happened to be needed elsewhere. He immediately saw the big deputy about fifty yards away, next to the popcorn stand, and it looked as if he was giving an earful to someone Cal didn't recognize from this distance.

He approached, and Jake saw him, waving one hand, while his companion headed off in the other direction. A few people came up to Cal and asked how he was, and he tried being affable enough, although in no mood for lengthy conversation. It took him longer than he thought to reach Jake, hearing a complaint or two along the way.

"What's going on here?" Cal asked.

"Not much, really. All the usual suspects out. No trouble though."

"Well, that's good." He paused for a moment. "I had a surprise visitor at the station." "Oh?" Jake's eyes lit up.

"A blue Nova was parked outside, revving the engine like it wanted to race."

In the twilight, Jake's face was unreadable. "You're kidding me."

"Nope. Right down the street. And I saw the same car earlier at the parade."

"You did?"

"Yeah, but there was nothing I could do. It was parked on a side street and I happened to see it in my rear-view mirror. It seems our elusive suspect has come out in the open now, throwing down the gauntlet in our faces."

Jake looked startled, which was rare for the brash deputy. Cal mulled over the implications of what he had just said, and it *was* a bit alarming.

Assuming it was Carson, was the guy now prepared to take things up a notch? But how far would he go in getting his point across? If he had just spent time in prison, would he be in that much of a rush to get back?

Probably not, although revenge did drastic things to people who let it consume them, and that was a concern. He'd seen this happen before, and it could ultimately lead to violence, suicide, and even murder.

Jake looked as if he were thinking the same thing.

"Be on your toes, big time. I still think he's going to try something tomorrow. The fire department will be here, and I want to make sure those guys are alert, and not all half-drunk themselves. And for once, I'll tell you *this*, Jake. Don't be too easy on troublemakers. We need to be proactive here. I don't want a repeat of what Nick did. Anyone gets out of line, ticket them on the spot. And if they give you any problem they'll be spending a night in jail."

The deputy looked at him, but said nothing.

"Stay until after closing. Tell the night guard to be vigilant, and that I expect some trouble, but don't know in what form yet. Who is it, anyway?"

"Cliff."

Cal frowned. "Figures. That guy touches a drink and I want him replaced. I don't care who you call, understand?"

Jake nodded.

"All right, see you tomorrow, but call me at home if anything happens, or if our friend in the Nova shows up. Radio Marlin to be on the alert for it as well. See ya."

Cal turned and headed off, knowing that it was going to be a long day tomorrow.

Real long.

When he arrived home, Cal got out of his car and leaned wearily against it, breathing in the cool air and feeling the wind caress his face like a lost lover.

October and Halloween were in the air, with all the memories, sights, and sounds of the orange and black season with it. It had quietly emerged from the warm days of late summer, making its way into the valley and streets of Shington. Emotions tugged at him from every angle, leaving him with an empty feeling in his gut. Did it have to be this way, he asked himself? When would he be able to come to grips with it all? Shaking his head, he walked into the backyard instead of inside his house, preferring the rawness of the night to the warm and comfortable interior of his own home. He needed to clear some things up in his head first.

Cal tossed around all the events of the past and present, trying to work his way through it all. He was happily married to Mindy, the only true love of his life, living in his childhood town, with arguably the most prominent position in Shington, besides mayor. He believed himself to be a good person, but he had made mistakes in the past which haunted him. Guilt was a tough thing to live with, and if he could go back in time, turn the hands of the clock, he would have gladly done so a million times already.

But he couldn't, and wishful thinking was for fairytales, and little boys with cricket friends.

No, he must come to terms with his life, and his choices.

His future.

There was the uncertainty of his career, and whether he might end up being mayor. Winston was leaving, and there was no doubt on that matter. Hell, it looked like he had already left. So the question was if Cal would forego his job as sheriff, and take the helm of mayor, if asked. He was sure to be nominated, and was confident that the town would vote him in. He wasn't being brash at all, but knew the town and its people like the back of his hand. He was popular, plus no one else was really up for the job.

So...

The other thing. The one which he tried to avoid thinking about. His involvement in something which had been harmful to someone else. Cal moved deeper into the backyard, melting in with the shadows, but he never had time to finish his train of thought as something emerged from the bushes and came toward him.

He gasped in surprise, his hand moving instinctively to his weapon.

"You won't need that, sheriff."

Recognizing the voice, and moments later the familiar outline, Cal narrowed his eyes in suspicion, his hand now resting on the hilt of his gun but feeling no less reassured.

It was Cass.

"What the hell are you doing here?" Cal asked. "I could have shot you."

"Maybe you could have." The girl shrugged. "But that's an odd question, since you've been looking for me all day. So… here I am."

Cal stayed alert, oblivious to what game she was playing. Her appearance now had multiple implications, but it was impossible to discover her motivation until he let her talk first.

"I can see that." He pulled out his flashlight, unwilling to let his guard down.

"I know you don't trust me, and I can't blame you for that. It's all my fault."

Cal frowned, puzzled by her change of attitude.

Cass spoke again, her hands folded in front of her, revealing them to be empty, which Cal figured was an intentional sign of peace. "You can arrest me now, if you like. I'll come willingly." Cal was silent.

"Even though I'm not guilty of what you might think."

"That remains to be seen," he answered.

"Regardless of what you do with me, it won't change the actions of others."

"Really? And what about Carson? Are you admitting to me that you've seen him?"

"Yes."

Cal was silent. Finally, the proof that he'd been waiting for. So Carson *had* returned to town after all his speculation. He was sure that he'd seen him in the Nova several times, and also that he was behind all the trouble. It was the break he'd been looking for. Yet it still didn't make any sense. Why was she here now, after threatening him the other night, and being so antagonistic when they had spoken before? It didn't add up.

Cal remained holding the flashlight, analyzing her mood and expressions. "And if you've seen him, then you've talked to him as well."

"I have."

Cal grunted, trying to wade through the strange conversation. "You're practically confessing to me. I know he's behind all the trouble. And if *you* knew this, then you're guilty by association or at least guilty of withholding evidence."

Cass shook her head in response. "I haven't talked with him about any of that. I don't know if he did those things or not. That's not why he came to me."

"And you expect me to believe you now, after all this?"

She hesitated, lifting her head, looking at him straight in the eyes. "I was wrong about you."

He listened to her words, wanting to find the sincerity, but then everything went black as something struck him from behind...

When Cal regained consciousness, the first sensation he had was of splitting pain, coming from the back of his head. His temple throbbed, and he felt cramped, constricted somehow. His eyes fluttered, and he was sure that they were open, but all he saw was blackness. What the hell? Groaning, he tried moving about, panicking for a moment when he realized he was in an enclosure of some kind.

"Ugh…"

He shifted around, trying to figure out what had happened, and where he was.

"You can't get out."

A voice spoke from somewhere close, deep and muffled. He didn't recognize it.

"I'll be back for you later, but by then, things will be over."

The words were chilling.

"I'll let you know the details before I take care of you too. You've had a decent career at being sheriff and running Shington, but the winds of change are in the air. The Celebration is almost here. Good bye, for now."

"Bastard. Let me out!"

He cursed, but realized that things had taken a drastic turn for the worse. His assailant had gone to great lengths to put him out of commission, and wasn't about to back down after taking him captive. He yelled a few more times, but was greeted only by a dead silence. He rested for a while, realizing that he was in the trunk of a car, most likely his own cruiser.

How was he going to get out of this?

Cal moved about, trying to make himself more comfortable, which was nearly impossible. The air was tight, but he didn't think he was in danger of suffocating for a while. He had to admit, his situation looked desperate. He had no idea where he was, and that meant nobody else did either. He also didn't know how long he'd been unconscious. It could easily have been hours. His head hurt pretty badly, and he feared that he might have suffered a concussion. He pushed on the trunk above him, but it was no use. It wouldn't budge. Feeling around in his pockets, he hoped to find his radio, although he was sure it had been taken from him. Seconds later he confirmed that, and also discovered that everything else was gone.

He then panicked for a moment, and it was a terrible time for him. He felt betrayed, knowing that Cass had set him up, playing him for a fool.

Damn, how could he have let himself fall for it?

Weary and sore, he realized that he should remain awake, suffering from a head injury of unknown extent. He tried to stay conscious, but found himself drifting away, his stomach empty, his throat parched, and his head beating drumlike in a slow cadence of pain. His memory of that time period was blurry, and he lost himself for a while in nightmares, where he felt trapped in place, unable to move, as terrible creatures descended on the town, moving steadily toward the center where the Celebration was taking place. He moved in and out of the dream, at times not knowing whether he was awake or not. His frustration continued to mount, and then a glimmer of hope appeared, as he remembered the small compartment in the trunk where he kept an extra gun. Feeling around, he found the casing, only to discover that it had been compromised, the weapon gone.

He swore, realizing that his assailant had beaten him. The irony of his situation was hard to swallow, being trapped inside his own vehicle, helpless and desperate. Cal feared what might happen to the town

with him out of the picture, the citizens of Shington
unaware of the danger they were in. Yes, his officers
would come searching for him, but since it had been
night, with no one around, there was little hope he
would be found anytime soon. Mindy would of course
have called him, and then the others, so all his men
would be on the hunt.

But where was he? And what time was it?

Cal had no answers, and none appeared to be
coming to light soon enough to give him hope. He
waited, and drifted into a restless slumber.

His worst fears had come to pass, and he
couldn't have found himself in a situation direr than this
one…

Cal first heard the voices in his dream, in that
murky state of consciousness between sleep and
wakefulness. The words were muffled, and he tried to
answer, but it felt as if his head was underwater, no
sound coming out. He became frantic, attempting to
make contact with this unknown person, and then he
realized that he *was* awake, and not still captured within
the wings of nightmare.

He listened, all his senses focused, and then he
heard someone speaking.

Pounding on the trunk, he yelled out. "Help me,
I'm in here!"

Pausing for a moment, he heard a response which
gave him hope.

The Celebration

"Is someone in there? Sheriff?"

"Yeah! Get me the hell out of here!"

"Hold on, hold on! Look for the keys."

Cal waited a moment, wondering who was out there, but it didn't really matter. *Someone* was there now, and he was sure it wasn't his captor, who had left, determined to go through with their threat.

"Cal, is that you locked in there?"

"Yeah! Who's out there?"

"Ramen."

What? he thought. *Ramen Grable, of all people?* "The keys aren't here. Listen. We'll see if we can pick the lock. If not, we got a crow bar, and should be able to get you out one way or the other. Just hold on tight."

"All right," he yelled back. "I can't really go anywhere at the moment."

Waiting impatiently, Cal heard them struggling outside for a minute or longer, and then without warning the lid popped open, and he found himself staring at Ramen Grable and both of the Bentley brothers. He grabbed the hands that were extended to him, and the men helped him out.

"What the hell happened to you? Looks like you're hurt."

Cal didn't know who was talking, and he leaned heavily on Ramen for support.

"Get him over to the truck."

The men led him to the bed, where they all but picked him up and sat him upright, although not roughly. A jug was put in his hand, and Ramen offered him a moist towel.

"It's my head. I was knocked out. How bad does it look?"

"Hmm. Skinned up pretty good. It's not a deep cut, but you still should see a doctor. Any idea of who did this to you?"

Cal blinked his eyes, trying to clear his head, noticing that it was nearly dark. "What time is it?" "Maybe close to six." Blake answered. "Damn. I've been in there since last night?"

One of the men let out a low whistle. Ramen spoke. "Well, we don't get much news up here, but I imagine a lot of people have been looking for you."

Cal drank deeply, patting his head gently with the towel, but knew he had no time to waste, injury or not. The Celebration had begun by now, with or without him.

"You've got to drive me into town right away. It's an emergency."

"For sure. You want to see a doctor? We'll help you, of course."

"No, that can wait. We're going straight to the town square. And I need a gun. I'm sure mine is long gone."

"We can do that. Sure you'll be all right?" Ramen asked.

"I'm not sure of anything at the moment except that something terrible is going to happen if I don't prevent it." Ramen nodded. "Let's go then," was all he said.

The Celebration

The ride down the ridge was bumpy, and Cal winced at every knock, but there was nothing for it. His head felt a little better, although he turned down the whisky which was offered to him. The men had water with them and some snacks, and he ate them hungrily. But it was only moments later when he started asking questions.

"So how did you happen to find me? I'm lucky you were close by."

They were near the Point, and it made some sense, as it was normally an isolated part of the area.

Ramen fidgeted, giving him a nervous look, glancing back at the Bentley brothers in the rear seat. "Well, it's kinda' strange. We were out in the woods hunting and saw a light near the Point, so we came to check it out."

"A light? What do you mean?"

"Something flashed in the distance, and we didn't know what it was, or who it might be. Could have been one of our folks in trouble, you know?"

Cal was puzzled by his explanation, and pressed him further. "So you found the car, and me. But what about the light?"

"That's the damndest thing," Ramen replied. "There wasn't anything around which could have caused it."

"A reflection off the metal?"

"Nope, not a chance. It looked nothing like it."

Blake spoke. "And with all the other stuff happening, we weren't in a rush to come looking, but Ramen said so. Could be whoever did this to you was still snooping around, or came back to check."

153

Cal knew exactly what he meant. They had all witnessed the bizarre event at the Point, which no one could explain, although Jake had never trusted Ramen and his folk. So what had caused the light? Someone had led them to his whereabouts, surely a stroke of luck for Cal. So that person had to have had knowledge of his assault and captivity.

One conclusion was that two or more people were involved, but did one of them have a reason to let him be found? And if so, then why? Wouldn't it have been much easier to do it themselves than hope Ramen and his men would be close by?

Maybe not, if they wanted to stay out of it and keep their identity secret. More questions than answers...

They were now off the main foothills, but Cal had no means of communication. He could find a home and make calls to the police station and directly to the coordinators of the event, but would that be enough, to shut down the Celebration and clear everyone away? It made perfect sense though...The town would already be on edge with Sam missing and now himself out of the picture. Maybe the event had been cancelled already, but he doubted it. There were several prominent citizens who would be against such an action at all cost, and would throw their weight around even in his unexplained absence. Most likely a few would seize the opportunity to subtly discredit him. Popular or not, there were always people like that around.

They came to the first home but the driveway was empty, the place apparently deserted. Cal knew it would take a few minutes to get to the town square, and by the time he made the call and got there, nothing would have happened regardless. People would either refuse to leave or think that it was a Halloween joke.

The Celebration

Similar things had been tried in the past, for that matter. No, it would make no difference at this point. He would go straight to the event and try to prevent his tormentor from completing his threat. Impatient now, he urged Ramen to pick up the pace, and the man followed through without argument.

It was a strange alliance, he thought. *Driving along with Ramen Grable, who may not have been his enemy, but had never been someone to confide in by any measure. And now here they were, in such unforeseen circumstances, hurtling into the heart of Shington in the hopes of preventing something terrible from happening. He wondered how Mindy had held up. She must be worried sick. Well, he would have someone call her immediately.*

And then he felt his stomach tighten as he considered the unpleasant possibility that she had also been taken captive, or hurt. He ground his teeth together, watching as the streets and homes passed by as they drew closer to the town square. He formulated a quick plan, and nodded to himself.

"All right. We're almost there, and here's what I need you guys to do."

The men were silent.

"First, you have a handgun for me?"

Blake brought one out, giving it to him from the back seat. "It's not registered, but…"

"Just forget about it. As long as it's loaded, that's all I care about."

"Yeah, it is."

"When we get there, I want you to drive over to my house and make sure my wife is there."

Cal stared at Ramen, the man's face drawn in a curious expression. "You think she's in danger too?"

"I don't know. But I want you to tell her I'm all right, and stay with her until I get back. You hear me?"

"I'll do that. I know what it means to protect my kin. I have family in town tonight as well."

Cal nodded. "You know where my place is?"

"Yeah."

"Thanks for your help, Ramen. I know you think Nick is responsible, but I'll tell you now, there are *real* people who did this to me, and they're going to be held to task for their actions."

"There needs to be a stop to what's been going on. I don't know if you can make a difference or not." Ramen shrugged.

Cal had no answer for him, and no time. Moments later they entered the business part of town, and they passed a number of people out on the streets, both coming from and going toward the square. Nothing appeared out of the ordinary, and that was a good sign at least. Turning another corner, it became more congested, and several fire fighters were in the street, directing traffic and enforcing the parking restrictions.

"Pull right in there." Cal pointed to a spot as close as possible to the first stands and main tent. An angry fire fighter started waving madly in their direction and Cal opened the door, signaling Ramen to move off. "Keep her safe for me," he said. "I owe you one."

"You have my word, sheriff." And with that the truck rolled away, leaving him with his back turned as the fire fighter stormed up to him.

"What do you think you're doing…" He started to yell, but stopped when Cal turned around.

"Sheriff? Is that you? Everyone's been looking for you. Where you been?"

The Celebration

"I don't have time to explain." It was Riley, one of the younger men in the volunteer department. He grabbed him by the shoulder.

"Here's what I need you to do. Round up your men, and call my guys on the radio. Something bad is going down here."

Riley's eyes were wide, his head shaking in surprise.

"We need to get an orderly evacuation from here immediately, you understand?"

"Yeah, but what's going on?"

"Just do it. Now. And do you know where Jake is?"

"I saw him in the main tent earlier. He's been running things since you've been gone."

"All right."

Cal pushed him off, pointing to some of the other fighters, one who had noticed the conversation and Cal's appearance.

He went straight to the main tent, a number of people staring at him. He'd been gone long enough for word to get around, but he figured it wasn't a general manhunt yet, not for less than a day. Storming ahead, he waded through a throng of bodies, keeping his eyes open for anything which seemed out of place. Everything appeared normal, but that did little to comfort him. Whoever had taken him captive was nearby, planning some type of destruction or harm, and Cal wouldn't rest until the event was shut down and people were safe, and the son of a bitch who had caused all this grief was locked away.

He hurried through one of the entrances to the large tent, peering inside. There was another exit on the far side which was used to bring in the animals and equipment. His instincts told him that if there was trouble, this would be the most likely spot, as all the exhibits were on display. He passed by dozens of pumpkins, some with ribbons on them from the judging. Vegetables and flower collections were everywhere, nestled alongside baked goods, canned items, and business vendors. He reached the middle of the tent in moments, spotting a crowd of people. There was a large circle of spectators in the center, gathered around a curtain where the biggest exhibit was about to be announced. Every year several businesses vied for the grand prize, and the top three were revealed in the evening to be judged. Jackson Frey was there, along with a pair of women from the Shington Ladies Auxiliary. The man's voice squeaked over the microphone, accompanied by a modest amount of applause, the curtain now being drawn to reveal the top three competitors. Cal knew it would be difficult getting these people out of there during the middle of the event, but at this point in time he didn't care who got mad. He moved directly to the three hosts, a number of people looking at him in surprise.

But his interruption was short-lived as gasps of horror and several screams erupted from the crowd, fingers pointing at what was now exposed from behind the curtain.

In the center of an assortment of handmade crafts and autumn decorations sat a trio of scarecrows which had been erected between dozens of hay bales.

And as Cal caught a glimpse of the display, he realized that he was too late…

The Celebration

The scarecrows were not made of stuffed straw and old farm clothes, but something much more lifelike -- flesh and bone. Eyes from their faces stared wide and open at the crowd in a look of pure, final terror.

On the left end was Stan the coroner, his thin figure looking gaunt and even paler than in life. The mayor was in the middle, his jacket half open, exposing his midsection. And on the right was Cass, dressed in her habitual dark clothing, her life and vibrancy depleted.

Cal was as stunned and horrified as the crowd of people around him. One person fainted, as mothers and fathers covered children's faces, some of them running away from the nightmarish scene, stumbling into each other in their desperation to get away. Others stood there in mute silence, too shocked to speak.

Cal was too late, and his stomach did a slow roll as he felt nauseous. He choked bile from the back of his throat, the cold sweat of terror seeping through his clothing.

What monster could have done this? his mind screamed. *What sick and twisted person was capable of such cold-blooded murder?*

The mystery of the mayor's disappearance was now revealed, accompanied by two other victims, and despite his revulsion, his mind reeled with possible explanations and motives behind the heinous crime. Why Stan? And Cass too? He had considered her to be a suspect behind all the trouble, setting him up the night before to be taken out of the picture, while the foul deed had been done. She had been right there! *And now...now she was dead.*

But he had no time to think as his job wouldn't allow it. It was time to act.

"Cover that up!" He screamed at Jackson, who stood there in a daze, his hands trembling. Cal knew he would get no help from the man, so he ran over and closed the curtain himself, all the time yelling at people to get away from there and out to safety.

"Send some men in here *now!*" He shouted, as people began to move, their inaction given a kick start by his emotion-charged commands.

"Damn..." He swore, a terrible feeling of loss flooding through him, the horror in his gut having no easy release.

Who had done of all this? Why?

He looked up and down the aisles, spotting Jake's tall form several dozen yards near the other entrance. They locked gazes for one moment, and then a loud rumble echoed in from outside the tent. An engine revving.

"Bastard." Cal's jaw was clenched so tightly that his teeth hurt. "You'll pay for this..."

Seconds later the motor heaved, the unseen vehicle screeching away, and Cal knew with a sickening certainty that the past had now come full circle...

The Celebration

Things happened very quickly then.

Jake barreled away, heading for the back exit, Cal following on his heels, although hampered by fatigue and his injury. He screamed for Jake to wait for him but he stumbled into someone, both of them falling to the ground. The man paused for a moment, then he helped Cal to his feet.

"Sheriff, who did this? Why would they do such a thing?" The man sobbed.

But Cal had no answers, and Jake was already out of sight. "Get home and stay safe. Someone is going to answer for this…"

He surged ahead, leaving the man in his wake. Time seemed to drag as he finally reached the exit, and he watched in despair as a squad car peeled off, certainly Jake in pursuit.

"Dammit. Jake!" He wanted the murderer alive and intact, to face their crimes and receive their due punishment, but he feared that Jake would take the matter in his own hands.

Not that he completely blamed him, but he was the sheriff, sworn to uphold the law. And justice was coming swiftly…

He looked around and saw Jim Sticher, who seemed to be just arriving. The farmer waved, obviously ignorant of the situation.

"Jim, I need your truck. Police emergency."

Jim's eyebrows knotted together. "Sure, what's the problem?"

"No time for it. Keys." Cal held his hand out, and Jim dropped the set into his open palm. "People are dead. Including the mayor."

Jim's expression changed into one of shock, his jaw dropping wide.

"Get with some of the others and try to keep people from panicking. Work with the fire fighters. I need your help."

Cal patted him on the shoulder, leaving the stunned man behind and hurrying into his pickup. He fired the engine and started off, nearly colliding with another truck with a trailer dragging behind. The man driving it cursed at him, but Cal ignored the remark and gesture, thinking only that Jake was well ahead of him by now. He quickly made his way through the other parked vehicles, going east and away from all the commotion. Although there was no sign of Jake or the unseen assailant, Cal knew where they were all headed.

Away from town.

The Wyming Creek bridge and the main highway which led away from Shington. Just as it had been seven years ago.

Cal felt crushed for time, virtually helpless without his radio and any means of communicating. He knew the situation was bad, and he had a sinking feeling that Jake would manage to catch up with their elusive adversary, for better or for worse. His instincts warned him that the outcome was yet to be decided, and there might be more unpleasant surprises still in store for them.

He just knew it...

Racing along the roads, he soon was leaving the business area and moving into a residential section, where the homes dropped off, morphing into outlying properties and farmland. His mind raged with questions, a whirlwind of possibilities and few answers to be found.

Sam, Cass, and Stan. All dead.

The Celebration

What was the common thread which had tied their fates together in such a terrible end? What did the perpetrator have against them all? His notion of someone taking revenge for Nick's death had been solid, but now Cass? If Carson was guilty – and Cal was certain of it – then why her? She had loved Nick, even believing him to have returned in the past weeks from the grave, seeking to avenge those who had done him wrong. And Sam? He'd been in office when Nick had died. Stan had been the coroner. Cass was Nick's girlfriend. He continued his line of thought. *What about the graves which had been vandalized? Marshall Raes and Pete Swigler. The former being the sheriff at the time, and Pete owning a garage which did all the police work.*

So, the lot of them together had been directly involved with the circumstances of Nick's death. And Cal had been an officer as well. That did little to comfort him, knowing that the only survivors from the fateful group were himself and Jake, both of them now chasing down Nick's murdering avenger.

Avenger…

Of an accident? Or something else?

He didn't know that answer just yet, but he felt like he was driving headlong into the jaws of a deadly trap, and could do nothing about it.

The road meandered along and Cal floored it, knowing that he needed to keep focused. He was nearing the edge of town, with still neither vehicle in sight. Hopefully Jake would have the frame of mind to call in the state police, as opposed to taking it all on himself. They both knew that there was no way the cruiser would catch the Nova on the bigger highway. Impossible.

163

Trees edged the road to either side, and Cal knew that the Wyming Creek Bridge was just ahead. He went around a bend, the truck rumbling ahead for another quarter of a mile when the forest finally opened up, the bridge appearing before him. It was almost completely dark and he raced ahead, his foot slamming the brakes as he saw a car at the far end of the road.

It was Jake's cruiser...

...and parked off to one side, the big officer was standing there now, facing into the trees.

Cal stopped the truck, rushing out, but Jake never even turned to look, instead staring into the brush where a blue Nova sat, the front end smashed into a tree, the driver's head sticking partway through the windshield.

Cal already knew that it was Carson, and that he was dead.

He moved forward, the glare from his headlights giving him enough illumination to confirm what his instincts had told him.

Even with all the blood and glass, Cal identified him as Nick's older brother, now joining his younger sibling at the same spot of his death. *The irony was chilling...*

"It was right down here, remember?"

Jake's voice drifted to him, coming from the center of the bridge.

"Halloween night, seven years ago. It seems like yesterday."

"Jake..." Cal started, but the deputy continued to talk.

"You came here after Nick's car crashed. That Nova could really move."

Cal turned away from the tragic scene, heading toward his deputy. His figure was shrouded in shadows, leaning over the rail and gazing down into the creek below, which bubbled and lapped over rock and pebbles.

"It's over now. You guessed right that Carson was back."

"What happened?" Cal stopped several yards away from him.

"You mean just now? Or back then…"

Jake pivoted, turning fully towards him with a pistol in his hand pointing straight at Cal's head…

And Cal finally understood everything at that moment.

Well, almost everything. Jake's response had placed the missing pieces together.

"You kind of knew, didn't you? And don't try anything. You know how good of a shot I am. Put your hands in the air. Slowly"

"I'm unarmed." Cal lied, knowing that Jake was too clever to fall for it.

"Now." He stepped closer, his finger on the trigger, and Cal complied.

"I guess you feel that I owe you some answers, right?"

"It doesn't have to be like this, Jake."

"Hmm."

"Please put the gun down. I don't blame you for

Carson's death." Cal pleaded with him, trying to keep his voice steady.

"But what about Nick's? You know what happened. I think you have for a while, or you at least suspected. I shot the tire out, Pete helped conceal the evidence, and Marshall considered it fair justice, ridding the town of its number one punk. And even Sam knew about it, covering for all of us."

And that was it, Cal thought. *A cover-up by all of them.*

He felt a twinge of guilt himself. He had lingering questions at the time, but had never really pursued them, knowing that the town authorities had closed the book on the tragedy.

What did that make him in the end? Was there blood on his hands as well? He was sworn to uphold the law, and perhaps he'd failed in his oath.

But no, he wasn't about to condemn himself to that extent. He wasn't perfect, but would never have gone along with the cover-up of a murder.

"We've sworn to protect and serve, Jake. There's no other option."

The deputy grunted. "And that's exactly why you'll never leave here alive, Cal. You could have this town crawling at your fingertips, have anything you want. *Anyone* you want…"

Cal cringed at that one.

Jake laughed. "I know about your fling. What's the big deal? Mindy might have a different opinion, of course."

His words struck home, and hurt him bad. This was the one dark secret Cal carried with him, like an unseen scarlet letter over his own heart. Here was the reason he dreaded the fall and this time of year, the shadow of Halloween holding the truth of his own infidelity and poor judgment in its orange and black cloak. That one period of time when their marriage had been troubled, and Cal had found temporary comfort in the arms of another, never forgiving himself, and holding the guilt deep inside. During October and near Halloween were the worst times. The memories…

"Well, she knows now, anyway."

Cal glared at him, stunned. "What?"

"I told her last night, while we were looking for you. Told her that you were thinking about leaving her, and moving away with your new lover."

Cal was furious, forgetting the delicacy of his situation and moving forward a step, but Jake would have none of it.

"Don't move! If you want to end this sooner, take another step. Please."

"You bastard. Why would you want to do all of this to me? I've always treated you fairly."

"You were always *stupid*, Cal. And I want what you have. To be sheriff. And even mayor. The town needs someone with a firm hand, someday to be afraid of. *Me*. I should have been the one, not you."

"So you did all of this? I still don't understand."
Mindy, I'm so sorry. I'll never have the chance to tell you.

Jake leered down at him. "I'll make it quick, since we'll have company very soon. Carson returned to town, and I caught up with him early. He was behind most of the stuff, as you assumed. But he didn't kill those three. *I* did!" "I don't believe it."

"Doesn't matter what you believe, now does it? I had Carson under my wing, and let me tell you, that boy had some real tricks up his sleeve. Did you know that before he went to prison and got hooked on drugs, he was in California for awhile? He learned some interesting things working in Hollywood. Brought some toys back with him. So he didn't kill them, but that didn't make him any less of a bad guy. He really only wanted Cass, can you believe that one?"

Jake laughed, but Cal found no humor in the sound.

"Yeah, he had always wanted her, and that's why he left Shington. I told him he could have her, but only after helping me. Even after he raced away, he still had no idea of what happened to her. Poor girl...I had to kill her. She knew too much and especially about Carson. They were a liability to me and my plans. Now you're the only one left who knows anything. Carson will be blamed for all of the deaths. After all, he came back for revenge, and Cass refused his advances. Those were his motives. And our poor sheriff was his last victim."

"You're sick, Jake. You need help. Please put down the gun. We were always friends."

"Sorry, but I've come too far now. Time's up..."

Cal winced, feeling a wave of loss, fear, and regret tumble over him all at once. His head felt like it weighed a thousand pounds, and Jake's words sliced through his heart like an angry knife. It couldn't end like this, Cal thought. There was too much for him to do, too much to live for.

"Jake..." Cal pleaded, but the gun was unforgiving and final, pointed directly at his head.

Jake sneered. "See you on the other side."

As he spoke the last word, a loud rumbling came from the far side of the bridge and a flash of headlights splashed across the road as a vehicle approached. How it had come on them so quickly surprised them both, noiselessly and without warning. Cal immediately knew that this wasn't a part of Jake's plan, and he wondered who it was.

The car approached, and Jake looked undecided as to who he would shoot first…Cal hesitated only for a second, knowing that he had a chance to make a move here, but he stopped short as the outline of a car came into focus.

It was a blue Nova.

"What the hell…"

But Jake never finished his sentence as the vehicle blasted straight towards them. It was all Cal could do to get out of the way, diving to the edge and hanging onto the protective rail.

Jake may have been surprised but he had a hunter's instinct. He fired off a round in Cal's direction and dodged away from the Nova in the same moment. Cal screamed as a sharp pain pierced his right shoulder, and he felt himself being thrown over the side of the bridge into midair, plunging downwards. His world became black as he hurtled into the cold water, trying to keep his head above the current.

Then everything went dark…

"How do you feel?"

Cal opened his eyes, feeling wearier than he'd ever remembered. Strangely, he felt warm and comfortable, and it took him several long moments to realize that he was in a hospitable bed, staring up into Mindy's dreamy eyes.

Mindy? She was all right! Mindy...

He wondered in disbelief. *Was he dreaming?*

"You look like you're half asleep, and the drugs are making you tired. But the doctor said you'll be fine." Her smile was warm and genuine, and she kissed his hand. Immediately his eyes teared up, recalling the horrific events which had led him here. All those who were now dead, and Jake's monstrous plan to kill everyone in his way...

"What happened?" His voice was a whisper. *Had it all been just a terrible nightmare?*

"They found you at the bridge, if that's what you mean. With both Jake and Carson dead." "At the bridge?" He remembered being shot, and the dull ache in his shoulder confirmed it.

"You're lucky. The bullet only skimmed you. How's your head? You have a mild concussion, but that will be all right too, the doctors said."

Jake had shot him...Jake -- who had been the *real* one behind everything. All this time, and he'd never suspected it.

"You're a hero, you know. But they'll want to question you more once you're better. I don't know how you managed to pull this one off, Cal. No one can still believe it. Jake and Carson together."

"What do you mean?"

Mindy bent closer to him. "Are you sure you're up for this? You've been through a lot." She squeezed his hand, but he only nodded in reply, holding tightly. "Well, Carson left a note at the Celebration explaining that Jake had framed him into doing all the vandalism, his goal to get rid of you and the others. Jake told him that you were responsible for Nick's death, but Carson figured out the truth somehow. All he wanted was to take Cass away from Shington forever. I'm afraid that wish will never come true now. Poor girl."

Cal looked down, squeezing his wife's hand. He didn't know what to say, but he had to talk, knowing that his secret was out. It was time to try and repair the damage he'd done.

"I know that Jake told you..."

Mindy hushed him, her face growing sad. "I already knew. I've dealt with it." She looked down, averting her gaze.

Knew. She knew? How?

"Please...don't talk about that now. It hasn't been easy, believe me. I've been over it for a long time. All I care about is that you're all right. I love you."

Cal felt the tears come unbidden to his eyes, and he saw them trickle down Mindy's face as well. "I'm sorry, so sorry for what I did..."

She nodded. Neither of them spoke for long moments, and Cal felt a queasiness in the pit of his stomach from how he had hurt his wife. How stupid he'd been, how selfish. Swallowing heavily, Cal knew that he was a lucky man, in many ways. And although Mindy might have forgiven him, he didn't know that *he* could ever forgive himself. He would have to live with that regret, and hope that someday his conscience would relent, let the past settle down to a manageable level. Cal knew it had been a terrible mistake. He was only human, with every weakness that came with it, but regardless, there was no excuse for his behavior.

Cal finally brought up another question.

"And the bridge? What happened to Jake?"

Mindy appeared puzzled. "Don't you remember? You were shot, and they said Jake was run over by a car. They found you in the creek, washed up on shore."

But Cal remembered being swept away by the cold water, unconscious, with no recollection of swimming to the bank. His wife stared down at him. "Who killed Jake? They want to bring them in for questioning. Whoever was in that car saved your life."

Deep chills went down Cal's spine. The blue Nova. The driver of the Nova had killed Jake, and saved his own life as well.

No, he told himself. *Impossible. It couldn't have been...*

Could it?

It was a week before Halloween, and nearly a year had passed since the terrible events of the Celebration. The town had suffered badly, but had come through in the end. Even in the face of such evil and destruction, the town had survived. Shington would never be the same again, but that didn't mean people had given up living their lives.

The incident had gone through the full scrutiny of the state police and FBI, with Cal being held blameless in the entire episode. And as to the identity of the mysterious stranger who had appeared at the bridge, ultimately saving Cal's life? Nothing. The driver of the blue Nova had never been found.

The Celebration

Cal looked out over the Point, and it was the first time he'd stood there since being taken captive and locked in the trunk of his own cruiser. He was on his way to see Ramen Grable, and oddly enough, the two of them had become friends since last year, putting aside their past differences. Himself, Ramen, and the Bentley brothers were going out hunting soon.

It was all very ironic. No one would have ever predicted it. Strange, crazy, unlikely, but good.

The wind was cool against his face, and the air made him feel clean; alive. The valley and surrounding hills were fully enveloped in the season, and for the first time in many years Cal felt at peace with the time of year. He felt *whole* again.

Cal knew that his life was full of riches, but not from his career and personal belongings. True, he was well-off between his duties as sheriff and mayor, but he found himself spending a lot of time reaching out to those in need throughout the community, and involving himself in every charitable project, both large and small. He had learned from his past mistakes. Learned and grown. But without Mindy at his side, he would have been much less of a man, and he readily admitted it. They had grown stronger as a couple in the past year, and Cal knew that nothing would ever make him drift away from her again.

Never...

He looked at the colors surrounding him. Burnt orange and yellow, wholesome greens and brown. This was his home, and would always be his home.

His, and Mindy's. Along with their newborn daughter.

A smile creased his face. Yes, home for them all. And someone else called this place home, although there

173

was no visible sign of his presence. True, there had been no more strange events like the past year. No more sightings, rumors, figures in the dark, silhouettes in graveyards.

No blue Nova's...

But that didn't mean *he* wasn't here, in some unexplainable way. Cal felt Nick's presence in the trees and hills, silent but powerful, and knew that he was out there somewhere, watching. Hopefully at peace.

Yes, Cal had a completely different perspective on everything these days. An appreciation of all the good things and blessings he had in his life, and he was determined to share that with everyone, most especially his family.

For how could he not love this time of year most of all, when their own beautiful child shared a special connection with this wonderful season as well?

Why else would they have given her such a perfect, meaningful name?

Autumn.

The End

The Celebration